# GETAWAY!

The van roared into reverse, rushing away from them, its headlights on full beam. Bodie loosed off a shot through the back of the vehicle. Doyle's explosive shot starred the side window. Bullet proof glass!

The shattered side window was punched through and a gun barrel appeared. Doyle dived to one side as four quick shots spurted from the ground next to his foot.

Bodie pumped two shots into the van's front tyre. It slewed wildly, but kept travelling, smoke appearing from its rear tyres as it swerved and skidded.

Doyle appeared in the entrance way to the car park, raised his gun and carefully shot out each of the rear tyres. The van swerved and crashed into two huge dustbins.

'That's shaken them up a bit, I expect,' said Doyle.

They stepped towards the motionless van.

*Also by Ken Blake in Sphere Books:*

THE PROFESSIONALS 1: WHERE THE JUNGLE ENDS
THE PROFESSIONALS 2: LONG SHOT
THE PROFESSIONALS 3: STAKE OUT
THE PROFESSIONALS 4: HUNTER HUNTED
THE PROFESSIONALS 5: BLIND RUN
THE PROFESSIONALS 6: FALL GIRL
THE PROFESSIONALS 7: HIDING TO NOTHING
THE PROFESSIONALS 8: DEAD RECKONING
THE PROFESSIONALS 9: NO STONE
THE PROFESSIONALS 10: CRY WOLF
THE PROFESSIONALS 11: SPY PROBE
THE PROFESSIONALS 12: FOXHOLE
THE PROFESSIONALS 13: THE UNTOUCHABLES
THE PROFESSIONALS 14: OPERATION SUSIE

# THE PROFESSIONALS:
# *You'll Be All Right*

**KEN BLAKE**

Based on the original screenplays by
**Gerry O'Hara and Christopher Wicking**

SPHERE BOOKS LIMITED
30/32 Gray's Inn Road, London WC1X 8JL

First published in Great Britain by
Sphere Books Ltd 1982


TRADE
MARK



Set in Plantin

Printed and bound in Great Britain by
Hunt Barnard Printing Ltd., Aylesbury, Bucks.

## *Chapter One*

The cat had finished with its night hunt, and came padding silently back to its home territory. It crossed garages, gardens and pavements, stopping every few moments to sniff the air.

Dawn was approaching. Images of food drew it onwards to the tall, detached house at the end of the street; thoughts of petting and cuddling from its playful, pleasant owners made it scamper through the shadows.

It was a family cat, plump, well-groomed, well loved by the children of the house. Lazy by day, at night it was transformed into a sleek hunting machine, exhibiting a savagery that might have shocked its innocent owners.

In this way, although it could not have considered the fact, it was very like the man who waited in the shadows of its home territory. The cat was aware of the figure, suspicious of it. Warily, it approached by a more circuitous route, stopping to watch the dark shape, trying to scent the aroma of the human on the crisp, dawn air.

The sky was brightening, the shadows lifting. The drab terraced buildings, backed by cluttered gardens and ramshackle sheds, seemed still, peaceful, almost uninhabited at this early hour. The cat knew every crumbling brick, every rotting piece of fencing, every dustbin-lined alleyway. It scampered towards the cat door that would give it access to the bigger house at the end of the row, but suddenly it stopped.

It had smelled blood, fresh blood.

The man in the shadows waved something green and glistening, and the waft of entrails touched the cat's sensitive nostrils and made it sit up and watch the stranger. After a moment, curiosity and hunger got the better of it, and it walked easily, almost indifferently, towards the dark corner where the fresh meat beckoned.

When the bloody offal was slapped onto the concrete path before it, the cat hesitated only briefly before running towards this welcome offering, and beginning to chew greedily at the soft, tasty guts.

It was so absorbed in its feast that it ignored the soft approach of the man who had treated it so kindly, and could do no more than scratch and struggle as it was grasped by the neck, and lifted from the ground, its belly exposed to the flashing steel blade of a fish knife.

She slept through the alarm and woke abruptly at seven-thirty, swearing loudly as she almost flung herself out of the bed, and reached for her house-coat. At thirty-two years of age, Chrissie Stone could take the occasional shock to her system, but this was the fourth time in two weeks that she had slept late, and it was beginning to get her down.

She walked quickly along the landing to the bathroom, knocking on the doors to the children's rooms as she went. 'Nick! Linda! Get up. Now! You'll be late.'

She heard the vague, childish sounds of protest as she closed the bathroom door and ran hot water into the sink.

Minutes later she was in the kitchen, frantically preparing a pot of tea, slices of toast and three bowls of cornflakes. Anne Hanvey would be here before she knew it, to pick up Nick and Linda for school. It was Anne's turn in the car, driving the five garrulous and argumentative children from the neighbourhood to St Michael's, three miles away.

'Where are you?' she shouted, and heard Linda come thumping down the stairs. Without looking at her as she burst into the kitchen, Chrissie said, 'Socks!'

The girl never pulled up her ankle socks. She was eleven years old, pretty, in a chubby sort of way, and quite bright. But she never pulled up her ankle socks, and it drove her mother to distraction. 'Where's Nick?'

'Looking for his toothbrush,' said Linda with a giggle. 'He'll never find it.'

Chrissie had no time to reprimand the girl, or help the

poor seven-year-old boy search in the bathroom for his toothbrush, hidden no doubt in the airing cupboard, or out of reach. 'You really are a little beast at times,' she said to Linda. 'Get the milk from the doorstep, will you?'

Nick came clattering down the stairs, solemn-faced with irritation, and looking fit to kill his sister. But he said nothing, just sat down at the table, a pale-faced, freckled child, his school tie knotted to one side, and catching part of his collar.

Linda opened the front door for the milk, and stooped to pick up the bottles.

Her scream was sudden, penetrating and quite shocking.

For a second Chrissie just stood by the grill, half watching the toast, half frowning, glancing along the hallway to where Linda was standing, staring down the front garden path. When the girl shrieked, 'Mummy!' she fairly ran to the front door, with a cry of, 'What is it? Oh God!'

She dropped to her knees by the hysterical child, watching the tears flood from Linda's eyes, feeling the girl's body rack with grief. 'Suki . . . ' said the child through her sobs, and Chrissie turned to look into the garden.

'Oh no. Oh God, no . . . '

The cat had been laid out on the step, like an offering, scarcely recognisable as a grey tabby through the blood that matted its fur. There was a white envelope next to it.

Chrissie bundled her daughter back into the kitchen, trying to calm her down. Nick had grasped that something big was amiss, and when the truth became known, through Linda's crying, he too burst into tears.

Chrissie tried to calm the children. 'We'll get another kitten,' she said. 'It'll be all right . . . '

Not to be placated, Nick became almost distraught. Breakfast was forgotten. A few minutes later, Chrissie had moved the cat's body round to the back of the house, and was escorting her two weeping children down the garden to where Anne Hanvey waited in the school car.

The car was already shaking to the fighting and teasing of the other three children, but a subdued, respectful hush entered the vehicle as Linda and Nick were bundled in.

'What on earth's happened?' asked Anne, anxiously.

Chrissie leaned down, placing the school lunches on Linda's lap and wiping at the girl's eyes with a handkerchief. 'It's Suki. She's dead.'

Anne said, 'Oh no! Was she run over? Oh Nick, Linda... I am sorry ... '

Chrissie said, 'I'll call you later and tell you. You'd better get the kids to school, now ... '

Linda abruptly stopped crying; her face hardened, and she almost snapped out, 'She was killed! Somebody killed her!'

Anne Hanvey looked startled, and questioned Chrissie silently with her glance. But Chrissie deliberately ignored her friend, reached into the back seat to dab at Nick's eyes with her handkerchief, and said, 'We'll get another cat. I promise you we'll get another.'

Taking her cue from this, Anne smiled at Nick, who was sitting tearful and sullen between the other silent, puzzled children. 'Of course you will. There, Nick, your Mum'll get you a nice little kitten.' To Chrissie: 'Is the puppy all right?'

Chrissie nodded.

'Don't want a kitten,' Nick said. 'Want Suki.'

One of Anne's children giggled, and Nick looked furious, the sound of the restrained laugh miraculously drying his tears. Chrissie closed the car door. 'Off you go,' she said to Linda through the window. 'Don't worry. We'll talk about it when you get home.'

As the car drove off, Chrissie stood in the street and watched it out of sight. She felt cold, and folded her arms across her chest as she walked slowly back to the house, looking down at the bloodstained front step.

With a quick nervous glance up and down the road, she stepped into the house and closed the door.

'What a disgusting thing to do,' she said aloud, as she walked through the silent house, picking up two items of Nick's clothing from where he had flung them *almost* into the utility room. She stopped, repeated, 'What a *disgusting* thing to do,' and realised that she was shaking like a leaf, and feeling close to tears herself.

The cat had been a family favourite. There could never be another Suki. But this was not the reason for Chrissie's restrained tears. 'She was the *kids'* cat. She belonged to *them*! Why hurt the kids? Why attack the kids? Bastard!'

She sat at the breakfast table, trying to calm her nerves, and eventually she drew the envelope from her housecoat pocket and opened it, reading the words that were written inside, and feeling the blood drain from her face.

*What are we going to do? Oh Dear God, what are we going to do? Jack can't take this pressure ...*

There was a distant sound, like the vibrating of pipes, or the sound of an air-bubble knocking through the central-heating system. Chrissie glanced up towards the ceiling, then back at the note. She didn't know what to do for the best. But the cat ... that was too much. It was the first violent act, and she knew the sort of man who had perpetrated that act far too well to naively believe that the slaughtering of Suki would be the beginning *and* the end.

Nick and Linda were one step closer to being in danger themselves, and something had to be done. Something positive. Something final. And now!

She tugged her housecoat tighter around her body, poured a large mug of sweet tea, and began to climb the stairs. She and the children inhabited the first landing, which was brightly decorated, and clean. But this was one of those large, Victorian houses than seem to have endless flights of stairs leading off from each level. On the second landing were two large, empty rooms, used as guest rooms and workshops. The place smelled musty and deserted, unmaintained.

On what Chrissie Stone earned, it was hard enough maintaining the bathroom, let alone the whole five-bedroomed monstrosity of the house in East London.

On the landing itself, pushed hard against a wall, stood a large, heavy wardrobe, ugly and bulky, the sort of furniture that Chrissie hated. She placed the mug of tea on the floor, opened the door of the wardrobe, and pulled out the toys, clothes and boxes that were crammed inside. Reaching to the back of the cabinet, she removed the rear panel, and tapped twice on the hardboard wall beyond. After a moment she tapped again, then stepped back to fetch the tea.

A section of the hardboard wall was tugged aside, and Chrissie glimpsed the pale, unshaven features of the man who lived in the concealed room.

'About time,' she heard the soft voice say, and stepped cautiously through the wardrobe and into the cold, spartan cell beyond.

'Good morning, Jack.'

'Is it? I'm freezing fit to perish. Christ, this place is miserable. Cold . . . '

'I know. It won't be for long. I've brought you some tea.'

Jack Stone took the mug from his wife, and sipped it gratefully. Chrissie sat down on the bare floorboards, and watched the haggard features of the man she loved.

Jack Stone was two years younger than her, but he looked ten years older. His black hair was well streaked with grey, and she could see white streaks in his beard as well, as his stubble grew thick and unkempt. His eyes were hollow, dark rimmed with fatigue and worry; his skin was unnaturally pale, the skin of a man who has been kept too long from the light.

Chrissie felt a moment's deep despair as she stared at her husband and realised, again, that he was slipping. He was letting go. The pressure was becoming too much for him, and though at first they had taken the challenge with both hands, and had almost made a joke of it, now the months of confinement and running, running and confinement, the eternal hiding, were beginning to take their toll of his spirit.

When the spirit flags, the body follows, and Jack Stone was literally draining away with despair and fear.

And who could blame him? This hidey-hole in the house may have been cunningly and expertly contrived, but it was a bleak and dismal place for a man of thirty to live in. Lit by a single, battery powered lamp hung from the exposed rafters, even with the bits of carpet and drapes hung down the walls the place was a prison cell, and felt like it.

As Jack finished the tea he said, 'What was all the yelling about? Thought someone was being murdered.'

'Someone was. Suki.'

'Suki? The damned cat?' Jack's brow furrowed, but a touch of bright fear had entered his eyes.

'The cat,' Chrissie agreed. 'Poor little thing. The kids are hopelessly upset. It's going to be a bad couple of days.'

Jack thought hard for a moment, almost not liking to confirm his suspicion. 'How was it . . . run over? Someone run it over?'

Chrissie took the sheet of paper from her pocket, and shook her head. 'She was cut open. Left on the step.' She was shaking again, the image of the cat's disembowelled corpse twisting her up with revulsion. 'This was propped up against the body, on the front doorstep.'

Jack took the piece of paper, his gaze not leaving Chrissie's, as if he was seeking some confirmation that the note was harmless. Chrissie just stared at him, and after a moment Jack read the contents of the note aloud.

'One, two, three, four, five . . . you'll be all right . . . you'll have something to remember, a lot to remember . . . one, two, three, four, five . . . But you'll be all right . . . '

By the time he had finished slowly reading his face was wet with sweat, his body hunched even more than before. He stared down at the paper, repeating softly, 'You'll be all right. All right.'

Then he crushed the paper in his hand, making a fist with which he struck once, twice, three times at the floor, saying with each blow, 'Damn! Damn! Damn!'

'Easy, Jack. Take it easy.'

'Take it easy!' His eyes were wide, wild. He held the crumpled ball of paper towards her, shaking his head. 'One, two, three, four, five! I'll be all right! Take it easy!'

'Let's get out of here, Jack. Let's go downstairs.'

He flung the ball of paper across the tiny room, picked up a tin mug with his shaving stick and soap inside it, and followed Chrissie through onto the landing. She was glad to see that he had decided to remove the untidy growth of beard.

'I'll make some breakfast, Jack. You go and freshen up. Look after yourself a bit.' She took his arm, tugged him towards her, and after a second his gaunt gaze turned on her and he smiled weakly, and kissed her brow.

'See anybody outside?'

She shook her head. 'Stay in the bathroom, and on the landing. Don't come down to the kitchen. I'll bring your breakfast up.'

'Take a look outside, Chris. See if you can see anyone.'

'Okay,' she walked with him down to the first landing. He was terrified, and his fear began to obsess her, so that she felt her own body begin to knot up with tension again. 'What are we going to do, Jack?' She wanted to weep on his chest, she felt so helpless. But with Jack a hunted man, she had to remain strong, certain. She had to be a prop for him to lean on when his own despair grew too great.

'I've got to make a call. It's my only hope.' They stopped, half way down the stairs, and Chrissie looked up at him, frowning.

'What do you mean, a call? Where?'

'Tonight. It'll have to be tonight. I'd better have my walk. I'll have to take the chance, love. It's all there is to it. A walk. Tonight. And a call ... ' he wiped his hand across his face, looking down at the moisture he rubbed off and laughing almost ironically. 'Look at that, Chris. Jack Stone. The hard man. Melting like a wax doll.'

She jerked his attention back to her. 'What call, Jack? Who have you got to call?'

'Someone who owes me.' There was an edge of bitterness in his voice.

'Who, Jack?'

'A moralising son of a bitch called Doyle ... '

'Ray Doyle? Jack, you can't!'

'Chris, I've got no choice. Do you think I *like* having to do this? Christ!' He walked stiffly, angrily down the stairs, and slammed the bathroom door behind him. The last thing Chrissie heard was that name again, spoken like an expletive. 'Ray Doyle!'

# *Chapter Two*

It never fails! Ray Doyle thought bitterly as the telephone began to ring, jarringly loud, across the room. He had just sat down in front of the television, beer in one hand, chicken leg in the other, feet on the coffee table, and Sportsnight just started.

He shook his head, smiling ironically, then took a quick swig from the can, before turning down the volume of the TV and picking up the phone. It had been one of those days when everything had gone wrong: the stake-out at the Saudi Embassy had produced exactly nothing; a false alarm, and after six, agonisingly boring hours, Cowley had called through the most welcome of messages: Go home lads. Get some sleep.

The first time in weeks that Doyle had had the chance to lazily watch a football match, and almost immediately the phone goes. It had to be Control. Or Cowley. It *could* have been a personal call, but Doyle's sixth sense for trouble was registering so strongly, that he didn't even bother to hope.

He picked up the receiver, and without identifying himself just said, 'Couldn't you have let me have an hour? Just one, solitary hour?'

'Doyle?' Control's voice sounded confused. Ray Doyle sighed. There was no point in playing hard to get.

'Himself.'

'We've got a party on line wants your private number. He won't give us more than "Jack".'

'Just Jack?' Doyle lowered the beer can, slightly puzzled. Jack was a common enough name, but the sound of it, and the touch of mystery associated with the call, made the image of a man swim into Doyle's mind.

And a name. Stone.

Jack Stone.

'He gave no more than that? Just Jack?'

'That's it. We've got a trace on the call. Shall we act on it?'

Doyle said, 'No. Not if it's who I think it is.' If it *was* Jack Stone, then if he wanted Doyle's private number it was to ask for help. There would be no point in picking up a man – even a man who'd given CI5 the slip years before – when that man was coming to them. 'Give him my number.'

Doyle gulped beer, standing by the phone and watching the silent football. It looked like a dirty match.

A minute later the phone rang and he snatched the receiver up, almost smiling as he heard the unmistakable gravelly voice of his old adversary.

'Jack Stone! As I live and breathe. Jack Stone. Back from the dead.'

'Hello Doyle.'

The phone call finished, Jack Stone buttoned up his heavy jacket and stood in the darkened box, for a moment, peering through the windows at the desolate streets around him. He had taken the bulb out of its socket in the telephone booth, nervous about being seen.

Now he stepped into the street, head down, and began to trot quickly back towards his house, about half a mile away. Every few paces he glanced back across his shoulder. His breath frosted slightly in the crisp night air.

The car turned into the road ahead of him, catching him in the full beam of its headlights. Stone gasped, stood rooted to the spot, listening to the engine revving up. The car was a wide-bodied machine, and he thought he could see the unmistakable markings of a Mercedes.

He turned and ran, darting to the side of the road, aware that the car had accelerated in pursuit.

He had expected something like this, and had picked his spot to call Doyle very carefully. He ran down the first alleyway he came to, across the next street, over gardens and waste ground, and finally slowed to a stop, listening to the still night. He could hear the car, distantly, and after a few seconds the sound of its motor faded away.

With a smile on his face he leaned forward, hands on his knees, to catch his breath.

Funny thing was, he thought to himself, as he walked back to his own house, they might not have been after me at all. But there was no point in taking chances.

He moved on quickly, then, and paused by a parked car, fifty yards from his own, darkened house. Across the street one of his neighbours was leaning out of a bedroom window, calling for her cat. After a moment she disappeared inside and the curtains were pulled across the light. With a glance around, Stone padded silently round to the back gardens, and approached his garage from the rear. He unlocked the small side door and stepped into the darkness. Pulling out a small pen torch he illuminated Chrissie's small car, its green paintwork dulled with dust and the fact that she hadn't cleaned or waxed it for months.

As he turned the torch towards the door to the house, he gasped with horror, then screwed up his eyes for a moment, thinking of his kids, before letting his gaze rest again on the ghastly thing that dangled before him.

'Bastards!' he said loudly, and repeated the oath as he reached up to untie the string that held the body of the puppy. 'What the hell did they have to do that for?'

And feeling sick, and shaken, he placed the dead animal in a piece of sacking and went into the house.

The cat, the dog ... what next?

What would they do next to try and get Jack Stone out of hiding?

Which of his kids ... ?

Ray Doyle led the way through what Bodie had immediately termed 'dilapidated suburbia'. They were away from the main road, walking briskly across cul-de-sacs, and through the small, linking passageways, between the wide, high-fenced gardens of the area.

It was a bright, crisp dawn, and Doyle was hopeful of a bright, crisp day, without rain, and without the freezing winds that had made the previous days so miserable and debilitating. Stake-outs were bad enough at the best of times, but when the elements were hostile, the hours of silent watching could seem like weeks.

'That's the house.' Doyle indicated the tall building, just visible behind the scattered beech and ash trees that clustered at the bottom of every garden, and along the small roadways. Bodie acknowledged, and glanced coolly around, searching the estate for signs of stealthy movement like their own.

'Is he under surveillance?'

'He's sure of it. See anything?'

'Quiet as the grave,' said Bodie, ignoring the repetitive barking of a dog, somewhere. As he spoke, so a radio started up, tuned to a rock station. The music was muted and distant, and did nothing to allay the sleepy, dawn feeling of the area.

They crouched at the bottom of Stone's garden, then went in through the gate, bent low, finding cover in the vegetable area, among the canes and wire netting, then darting to a position behind a tall, trellis fence.

A window in a nearby house opened, and Doyle watched an old lady lean out, look around, then pull back inside.

Beyond the fence, someone was in the garden, digging. Doyle rose to full height, stepping out across the grass, and saw Jack Stone himself, crouched by the flower border, a trowel in hand. He was just covering earth over something he had buried. He looked tired, dishevelled, very pale.

Doyle glanced back at Bodie, and made a slight motion with his head. Bodie rose to his feet, too, and stepped into the lawn area, pushing the rusting child's swing so that it creaked slightly.

Stone glanced up sharply.

'Hello Jack,' said Doyle, and watched as the man looked anxiously beyond the two CI5 men, then over the neighbouring fence. He rose to his feet, wiped his hands on his jeans, then beckoned them to follow him up to the house.

'He's nervous,' said Bodie, as he and Doyle trotted across the cracked patio and into the house through the back door. There was a smell of fresh coffee in the kitchen, which made

Doyle's mouth water. A thin, solemn-faced woman stood by the stove. She was dressed in a towelling robe, and had her arms crossed defensively. 'Morning,' said Doyle pleasantly, but no smile touched her attractive features. She cocked her head towards the hall, and Ray Doyle led the way into the lounge, where Jack Stone stood by the window, peering round the curtains at the street outside.

'We came the back way,' said Doyle.

'No one in sight,' said Bodie. 'Unwind, Jack.'

Stone made a sound like a snigger, glanced at Bodie almost contemptuously. He walked back into the lounge, picked up a bottle half full with scotch, and poured himself a liberal glass full. He raised the bottle towards Doyle: you want a drink? Doyle shook his head. Bodie just stared at the man, his smooth features touched with sour disdain.

'Sit down,' said Stone, after he had taken a large mouthful of the whisky. He seemed to find the spirit relaxing, and sat down himself, crossing his legs almost casually. Bodie walked to the window, while Doyle took a seat on the arm of the settee.

'Where'd you spring from, Jack? Out of the grave?'

Stone said nothing for a moment, staring at the CI5 man, perhaps still not sure of whether or not he was doing the right thing. He sipped his scotch, then said, 'All over the place. Here and there ... everywhere.'

Bodie looked over at him. 'Glad to see us Jack?'

'Not particularly. Got no choice.'

'So what's that in the garden? A nice little bit of burying going on. Couldn't be ... surely not ... ' Bodie glanced at Doyle, who finished: 'The loot? Burying the loot?' He glanced back at Bodie, 'Not our Jack. Too canny for that. Got it salted away nicely, in Switzerland, I expect. Nice little wind-fall ... if he can ever get to it.'

Stone said nothing, just stared at Doyle, whose boyish features looked hard, baiting. Doyle's pale eyes gleamed, a touch of triumph, a touch of hostility.

'So what *were* you burying, Jack?'

Stone said, 'The dog. Eight months old, a Spaniel pup. The kids will be heartbroken. Yesterday the cat, now the dog. I don't know what I'm going to tell them. Heart-broken.'

'Unnatural causes, I take it,' said Doyle, and Stone nodded grimly.

'Head bashed in. Poisoned first, I think. Savages! Bastards!'

'I'm sorry for them,' said Doyle. 'The kids. They deserve better. Than you.' Stone scowled, but made no retort.

Bodie leaned against the wall, hands hooked into the pockets of his jeans. 'How long have you been here, Jack?'

'What's the difference? A few months. Maybe more.'

Ray Doyle cocked his head. 'A lot of people looked for you for a long time. Australia. South America. Mediterranean. We thought you were long gone and far away. And here you are, in your own house, and looking like you've just come out of solitary.'

'You're the last one, Jack,' said Bodie with a thin smile. 'The Last of the Mohicans.'

'The others are all locked away. Every one of them. All but Jack Stone. You're a regular Houdini.'

Stone had tired of the gentle baiting. 'All right, leave it out. Don't need all the clever, clever, not now, not with what's happening to me ... '

Doyle allowed an expression of mock sympathy to touch his features. Then he said, 'You asked for me, Jack, and here I am. I've come to take you in. I could just as easily send the Boys in Blue. You're big business, Jack. Some inspector could have got his promotion over you ... DCI, Superintendent, big splash in the papers. But you asked for me, and I don't handle your kind any more. You're not in my class ... '

As he spoke, so Ray Doyle's voice hardened, and he stood up from the armchair, hoping that Jack Stone was getting the message: the favour was over. He had called for Doyle, and Doyle had turned the clock back, and come to make the arrest in person. But now it was time to go ...

Sensing that his two early-morning visitors had finished playing with him, Stone said, almost desperately. 'Listen, I didn't get you here just to take me in – '

'Oh what a shame,' said Bodie coldly. Stone gave him a withering, contemptuous look, then stared back at Doyle.

'It's my family. My family's being threatened. Not me, the family. It's a lot bigger than just being watched. They're going to go for my kids, or Chrissie, I just know it. Look at this. You've *got* to help me!'

He handed Ray Doyle the crumpled note, which Doyle accepted and read, before passing it to Bodie. 'I don't owe you a monkey's damn ... '

Stone began to get very edgy, his hand shaking as he held his whisky glass. 'I got no one else to turn to. Some bastard's rumbled I'm here – or thinks I am. Else they know I'm in touch with Chrissie.'

'And they've started to "take out" your family. They've hit the first ... '

Stone shook his head grimly, reminding Doyle about the cat the day before. 'On the front doorstep, splayed out like an offering. With that note.'

Bodie read aloud, 'One, two, three, four, five ... You'll be all right ... You'll have something to remember, a lot to remember. One, two, three, four, five ... But you'll be all right.' He glanced at Doyle. 'Doesn't scan.'

'Don't suppose it was Wordsworth who wrote it.'

Bodie looked down at Stone. 'One and Two they've got. Three is obvious, then. Who's the youngest child?'

'The boy. Nick.'

'Unless you do some fast remembering. So who's got it in for you? Whose nose did you rub in the dirt before you skipped the country?'

Chrissie came into the lounge, looking slight and fragile in her housecoat; she glanced nervously at the two CI5 men. 'I'm making a fresh pot of coffee ... '

'Yeah, lovely,' said Doyle, and Bodie smiled at her and nodded his head. 'And a biscuit, love. Ta.'

Stone placed the glass on the table, leaned back in his chair and eased his hands into the pockets of his jeans. 'Could be one or more of hundreds ... '

'Occupational hazard,' Bodie observed wearily.

'Some heavy money funded the job,' Stone went on. 'You don't do a bank like that one without some seed money. Maybe some weren't in at the share-out.'

'But you were. Jack Stone was there, getting his share, and more besides.' Doyle smiled as he remembered the job. He was talking about four years before, an eight-man team hitting the National Bank of America. It wasn't so much the cash, although there was plenty of that; it was the security boxes that had afforded the biggest haul, the accumulated assets, in gold and precious stones, of hundreds of Americans in England. And some of those Americans in England had been influential and important people.

Hence CI5's involvement, although it had been an assignment with an only partially successful outcome. Very little of the haul had ever been found. And Jack Stone had slipped the police and secret service web. CI5's fingers had closed on empty air.

Now here was Jack Stone again, a hunted, haunted man, pleading for his life, quite a contrast to the cool, calculating criminal who had led that bank team, years before.

Chrissie came in with a tray of coffee, biscuits and cups. She poured the coffee black, and left it for the three of them to add milk and sugar. As she walked to the door, Bodie said, 'Got a bit of cling film, polythene bag, something like that?' He waved the note by its very edge. Apart from the Stones' fingerprints, there might have been others on the paper, but the forensic lab liked all their bits and pieces presented in nice, clean polythene bags.

Doyle took his coffee black, sat again on the side of the armchair and sipped at the cup, staring at Jack Stone. 'You ripped them off, you ripped them off really bad. I don't wonder they're after you. Who were they, any idea? You must have got wind of a name or two . . . '

But Stone shook his head. 'I wasn't that high up. I don't know who funded the operation. I was just one of the technicians. We all knew each other, and we all had one contact, who we all knew quite well. That was it. "Word was sent", not delivered personally, and the same went for the seed money.'

Sounding irritated, Bodie said, 'But you don't deny you ripped them off!'

Jack Stone looked anguished, almost desperate. 'But I *do* deny it. We all got ripped off. You don't know what it's like.' Looking at Doyle, with whom he found more sympathy. 'Of course there was money there. Big money, and nice little boxes of uncut icicles. But the straightening and the fixing, the money changing, it cuts the value down to a fraction of its true worth. You know this, Doyle, you know how it works – '

He broke off abruptly, and Doyle glanced round as the sleepy shape of Stone's young son, Nick, entered the room. The boy was tousle-haired, and his pyjamas were crumpled. He rubbed his eyes as he stood there, staring at the two strangers. Bodie stayed solemn, but Doyle gave the child a quick smile. 'You're up early.'

Nick just stared at him, then looked at his father. Stone said, 'What're you doing up so early, son? Go back to bed for a while.'

'I heard you talking,' said the boy. 'I couldn't sleep.'

Stone stood up, swung the boy into his arms and kissed his cheek. 'You're still half asleep. We woke you up, didn't we? You go back to bed . . . '

'Who're these men?'

'They're some friends of mine. Haven't seen them for a long time. Go up to your room. I'll come up in a minute and bring you a cup of tea. Go on . . . '

He put Nick down, and the lad hitched his pyjama trousers and walked wearily out of the lounge. Doyle heard him saying to Chrissie, 'I want to stay down here, with Dad.'

'Not now, Nick. Dad's doing some business.' There was the sound of the boy clomping miserably up the stairs. Chrissie passed Bodie a polythene snapper bag, then left the room again. As he placed the scrap of paper into the bag, Bodie asked, 'The kids know you're back then. How long have they known that?'

'They don't, really. Chrissie and I pretend visits. I'm supposed to be away abroad on business, but sometimes they come home from school and surprise, surprise, here I am. Just for the night. Little presents, all that sort of thing. They're too glad to see me to worry about authenticity. But it's a strain ... '

As he strolled back to the front window, and peered behind the curtains again, Bodie asked, 'And where *were* you on all these exotic foreign trips?'

'Up in the bloody rafters,' said Stone grimly; he shivered, perhaps a response to the thoughts of having to go back up into the roof space, into the cold, cramped quarters.

Doyle was impressed. 'Right here on the spot?'

'Made a little room, secret entrance. Hardly space to stretch out. Look at me. I've not seen proper sun for months ...'

With a grin, Doyle said, 'I heard of a German bloke who kept one of our lads hidden for years after the War. Kidded him the war was still on, long after it had finished. You'd have been better off doing your time, Jack.'

'Yeah, maybe.'

Bodie said, 'How about your kids? Could they have blown it for you? You know how kids talk.'

But Stone shook his head slowly, definitely. 'No. Not in families like ours.' He glanced at Ray Doyle, who seemed to understand. 'You know that.'

'Yes I do.' Doyle abruptly got up, drained his coffee and placed the cup gently on the tray. He seemed to come to a decision and stared hard at Jack Stone. 'Listen, Jack, this is not for us ... '

'What d'you mean?'

'We'll turn you in, arrange police protection, perhaps the family'll have to move away for a while, but – '

'But they'll get done!' Stone rose to his feet, his voice reflecting the urgency in his body. He trembled, with rage, with panic. Bodie watched implacably from the window. 'You can't disappear a family!'

'Sorry, Jack.'

'You can't lock me away with that on my mind!'

Bodie said, 'You haven't got a lot of option.'

Stabbing a finger towards the note, which Bodie still held, Stone made a last desperate plea for a more individual assistance. 'That note. That's got to be some kind of a nutter. Ripping the cat. Smashing the dog's head in – I can't! I can't leave them like this!'

With a touch of genuine sympathy in his voice, Ray Doyle walked over to him and said, 'Jack. You don't have the cards. We've got to take you in – now.' He reached for Stone's arm, but the man jerked away, panic growing, his pallid features quite flushed, now, with the sense of growing desperation that made him behave so urgently.

'If I could find a few grand.' Looking from one to the other of them. 'A few thousand quid ... '

'Leave it out,' said Doyle.

Bodie snickered. 'So you have got some tucked away.'

'No I haven't. That's all long gone, my share of the haul. But Chrissie's Dad might put it up – not for me, for her. He's got a fair bit of savings.'

Again Doyle reached for Stone's arm, and this time Stone didn't resist. Doyle said, 'The money's out, Jack. And this is not our line.'

In a last effort, his voice subdued, depressed, Stone pleaded with Doyle. 'You could *make* it your line. I'm not asking, I'm *begging*. I'm begging for my family, not for myself. I'll do a deal with you, I expect that. But please, help me now. In your mob you make up your own rules, you can't deny that!'

Bodie laughed, and Ray Doyle's eyes twinkled with a momentary amusement. 'That's true I suppose ... '

'I wouldn't like the Boss to hear us talking like this,' added Bodie. When Doyle turned to him and said, 'What d'you think?' he just shrugged.

'Why not?'

Stone closed his eyes, and let the breath ease from his body. Doyle's grip on his arm grew stronger.

'Thank God,' the man said. 'Thank God for that.'

There was no question, of course, as to which of them would have to put the proposal for 'protection' to Cowley. Doyle had known Jack Stone before the bank job that had sent Stone to earth, and it was Ray Doyle, not Bodie, who Stone 'trusted', as much as he could ever trust anyone.

So at mid-day, Doyle was standing at the top of the wide, stone steps of St Paul's, waiting for the memorial service for a 'retired' member of MI5 to finish. The sound of deep singing died away, and as Doyle paced restlessly up and down in front of the Cathedral, he heard that noisy shuffling and murmur of conversation that told of the imminent debouchment of several hundred men and women of precise military bearing.

Within minutes the steps were swarming with black-coated, medal-encrusted figures, all on their way to raise double gins to the fond memory of the man who had been a leader in the game of Intelligence.

Doyle spotted Cowley, who made his way across to him. Cowley never looked anything less than dapper, in his long black greatcoat, bowler hat on head, umbrella carried over left arm, despite the chauffeured car that was waiting for him not more than a hundred yards away.

George Cowley: head of CI5, and a man who contrasted totally with his youthful, jeans-and-leather-jacket clad operative. But dissimilar though they were in appearances, they were alike – very alike – in the way they thought; precise, analytical, hard-edged, CI5 was a no-nonsense operation for no-nonsense men, and when the dirty tricks division of the Secret Service was asked to turn its hand to a 'favour', there had to be some tough negotiating by all concerned.

Ray Doyle had bowed to Jack Stone's pleading request for protection for his family. Now it was up to Doyle to convince Cowley.

They spoke briefly, and to the point, walking slowly towards the long, black limousine that would take Cowley back to CI5 headquarters.

Cowley was unhappy with what Doyle proposed, and his craggy, northern features frowned and flexed with irritation as his operative spoke.

But Cowley knew one thing about Doyle above all else: if Doyle had agreed to help Jack Stone, then he would help the man, with or without CI5's blessing.

'And then what?' Cowley asked, as Doyle finished his pitch. 'What happens ... after?'

'Then we bring him in. Or he turns himself in. It'll come down to the same thing.'

'Amazing.' Cowley stared into the distance, his eyes narrowed against the bright day. 'Locked himself in his own private prison.'

'With a few mod cons and ... well, amenities ... '

Cowley shook his head. 'Rather him than me ... even *with* the obvious amenity of his wife being accessible to him.'

With a smile, Doyle said, 'More ways of killing a cat ... '

But Cowley, with a sharp comment, wiped the smile from Doyle's boyish features. 'That's a joke in very bad taste.'

Glancing away, Doyle said apologetically, 'Thought you'd like a laugh – these solemn occasions, old friends dying.'

They reached the limousine. Cowley looked back up at the rising heights of St Paul's. 'Memorial service for a brave man. He lived a full and active life. Not a sad occasion at all. And he always enjoyed a laugh. He would probably have quite liked you, Doyle. You'd have appealed to his own spirit of mischief.'

'Thank you, sir,' said Doyle, not knowing what else to say.

Cowley said, 'I'm not entirely happy about this, about Jack Stone. It's not really our "bag", Doyle. You know that. But I'm seeing the Commissioner later this afternoon. I might just touch on it, our involvement ... '

Awkwardly, not liking the thought of too many people knowing about Stone's whereabouts, Doyle said, 'The fewer the better, sir. Don't you think?'

Cowley frowned. 'What are you implying, Doyle? That the Commissioner might not play the game?'

'I'm not implying anything, sir. They're nice kids, a boy and a girl. They deserve fair play, even if Stone doesn't. Maybe I should have turned it over to the locals ... '

'They may be nice kids,' said Cowley sharply, 'but that's a family with a pedigree of villainy on both sides. His wife's father – Len Hatch ... '

'The Hatchet. I know.' Doyle had experienced Len

Hatch when he had been a policeman on the beat. A tough customer, a man to be reckoned with. He was also an old man, now, and Doyle pointed this out.

'Mellowed too, no doubt,' added Cowley. 'They all do. Their criminal pasts become the "good old days", stories for the children. The violence is forgotten; the adventure and the romance of robbery is blown up. Fairy tales.' He paused, watching the dispersing crowds from the Cathedral. Then he turned back to Doyle, opening the door to the car at the same time. 'Well, you have my approval for now. Low profile. No big teams wrecking my budget! And I mean that. You're sure you got in and out of the house unobserved?'

'Yes sir. Quite sure.'

'Then carry on, Doyle. Report to me tomorrow.' And he ducked into the car, which swept silently away towards the city.

# *Chapter Three*

The moment Bodie received Doyle's 'go ahead' call, at shortly after mid-day, he went into action, and the first move was to contact Liz Spalding. He pinned her down at the CI5 computer centre, and over the phone briefly explained what he and Doyle needed of her.

She was furious. She had been on call for forty-eight hours, had snatched very little sleep, and was about to enjoy two full days leave. But Bodie softened his voice, teased Liz mercilessly, until she agreed to meet him a few minutes later, to be taken to Linda Stone's school.

Liz Spalding was in her early thirties, an attractive, red haired woman, and one of CI5's most devastating operatives. Bodie and Doyle were hard, and *looked* hard. Liz Spalding looked anything but the fighter that she was; she could get people off their guard, get their defences down, just by looking at them.

And when she moved in for the kill she was as hard, and as final, as any of her male colleagues.

Bodie was waiting for her as she trotted down the steps from the Centre, bag slung over one shoulder, slim body dressed in a bright blouse and pleated skirt. Bodie had always had a passion for the woman, and he smiled, eyes narrowed and watching appreciatively, as she walked towards him. The smile faded rapidly as she snapped, 'I hate men who look at me like that.'

'Sorry,' he said, then grinned again. 'But I like to be up front about these things.'

Ignoring him, Liz said, 'Bodie, this just is not on! I've just come *off* duty! I really don't want to start a whole new surveillance routine.'

'A favour,' said Bodie. 'Can't a fellah ask a favour once in a while?'

She stood defiantly in front of him, shaking her head, trying desperately to find the words to make him realise that she was tired, due for leave, and really felt he should ask someone else.

All she came up with was, 'Pose as a schoolteacher! A *schoolteacher*. God. Do I look like a schoolteacher?'

'More so than I do,' Bodie said evenly. 'I'd look ridiculous in skirt and brogues. You're the only person we can ask, Liz. Do us a favour. It won't be for long.'

Exasperatedly, she shook her head, watching the traffic. But she didn't turn away from Bodie, and he knew that she would go along with the request. 'I just don't look the part. I hope. God forbid . . . ' Glancing at him.

'Pull your hair back, put your spectacles on.'

'I don't *wear* spectacles.'

'Look, not all school teachers are middle aged and drab.'

'Mine were.'

'Mine weren't. I had an English teacher, every time she stood in front of the window you could see – '

Liz cut him off sharply. 'Don't say it, Bodie! I don't want to hear any feeble jokes about seeing every detail of her sentence constructions!'

'Declensions, actually.'

'You're a pig, Bodie. An irritating pig.'

'But lovable,' he said with a wry smile. Then, more seriously, 'Look, Ray Doyle's got himself involved – '

'Doyle! I might have known he'd be behind it.' She shook her head, almost in despair, then glanced at her watch. 'Forty-eight hours,' she said wearily. 'I need a bath, a decent meal, and a good long sleep. And here I am agreeing to pose as a bloody school ma'am.' She sighed exaggeratedly. 'I mean, what is this, official? Unofficial?'

Bodie had won her, and reached to take her arm, leading her to his car. 'Semi-official. Okay?'

'Okay,' she agreed, glumly.

'Seal it with a kiss?'

'I'd sooner kiss Cowley!'

As soon as he had driven Liz Spalding to her small apartment, where she made some basic changes to her appearance, and grabbed a bite to eat, Bodie took her to Linda's school. He left her at the gates of the modern-looking block, then drove to St Michael's, where Nicky Stone was a pupil.

St Michael's was an older building, almost entirely constructed of red brick. It brought back unpleasant memories, for Bodie, of long, tedious hours at a desk, learning the sort of things about Swedish Industry, and the difference between X and Y, that he would have far preferred to have left undiscovered. It was on the playing fields that he had excelled, and had felt most at home, and it was on the playing fields that he now spent the afternoon. Dressed in track-suit and running shoes, he took classes 4A and 4B, which included Nick Stone, through a vigorous programme of junior callisthenics.

The boys gasped, wheezed and giggled; the plumper ones complained bitterly. Bodie ignored the sounds of dissent. He was enjoying himself hugely; it was not at all bad, he thought by the end of the afternoon, not at all bad being a teacher.

After the games session, Bodie went to the main school building, and spoke with the headmaster, in the main study, which overlooked the front playing grounds.

The headmaster seemed young, to Bodie, for a man with responsibility for so many kids, but he was pleasant enough, and certainly co-operative, and was prepared to let Bodie act as deputy sports master for as long as the surveillance on young Nick Stone was needed. As the children spilled from class rooms and changing rooms, out onto the playground, where their parents waited, Bodie located Nick, and kept an eye on him.

The usual routine for the Stone family was that Chrissie, and two other mothers, alternated coming to pick up a total of five children every day. There were three girls, including Nick's sister Linda; the other lad was Nick's close friend, Louis Hanvey, with whom he now propped up the school wall, waiting for the 'school-run Mum' to arrive.

'Once he's been picked up,' Bodie said, 'I'll be off duty until the morning. Back here at nine.'

The headmaster said, with a smile, 'Why not come for assembly? You could read the lesson.'

'Er . . . nice idea, but I have to check in at CI5.'

'Oh what a shame,' said the teacher, a twinkle in his eye. Bodie shivered at the closeness of *that* escape, and glanced back to the wall where Nicky Stone was lounging.

There was no sign of him, or of his friend Louis!

Bodie flung himself to the window-sill, leaning hard up against the plate glass and searching to right and left of the playground. There were still several boys, waiting for their lifts home, and a number of cars were pulling out of the main gates. But Nick Stone was nowhere in evidence, and none of the departing cars were the models that Bodie had been primed to watch for.

'Oh Christ, they must have decided to walk!' he said angrily, and ran from the study. He flung himself down the marble stairs, and out through the front doors of the school. When he reached the gates, pushing through the children, he looked both ways along the main road, then set off at a trot in the general direction of the Stones' household, several miles away.

'We really ought to hang on.'

'Come *on*! She'll be ages yet.' Lou Hanvey was a persuasive child. When his freckled face screwed up with childish annoyance, it was hard not to notice him, or take notice of him. And Nicky Stone, his best friend, always did what Lou said. Louis was a year older than the Stone boy, and the difference in age between seven and eight is quite remarkable when seen through juvenile eyes.

Anne Hanvey was late. She had volunteered two days 'school run', but she was forever on the phone, and Louis was well used to the delays and lateness in the family caused by his mother's interminable phone conversations.

'If we *walk*,' he emphasised, to glum little Nicky, 'we can bounce the ball. And she's *got* to come past us anyway, so she'll see us won't she?'

'Okay!' Nicky hadn't thought of that. More cheerfully he trotted after Lou, catching the tennis ball as it came bouncing towards him. The road was quite busy, but the boys knew enough to keep well away from the kerb. They half ran, half dodged, in the general direction of home, playing their ball game, in blissful ignorance of the fact that Anne Hanvey was late because she had gone shopping first.

They could look out for Lou's mum all they liked, but they wouldn't see her. She had come the other way to the school, and was parked by the road, now, increasingly fretful that the two boys were nowhere to be seen.

After five minutes they were well away from the school, chasing along the road, laughing and yelling as they pitched the ball back and forth between them. They collided with a labourer, pushing a wheelbarrow of demolition debris, and he swore loudly at them as they scampered away. When the ball bounced into the street, Louis Hanvey darted after it, satchel swinging on his back, and a double-decker bus screeched to a halt, a few yards away. The driver leaned out of the window and shouted at the lad, sounded his horn twice, then drove on.

Louis was quite sobered by that, as all his kerb drill and road-sense instructions came back to him in his father's stern voice.

But within moments they were playing again. Nick Stone felt exhilarated with running, and though he was hungry, and vaguely thinking of beans on toast, he encouraged Lou to slow down, so that they could have more playing time together. If he was slightly puzzled as to why the familiar car that Louis's mother drove hadn't yet passed them, he put it from his mind as he enjoyed the walk home.

Some way ahead of them, turning into the main road, came a sleek grey Mercedes. Nick spotted it by the sudden flash of light on its chassis, then put it from his mind. There had been a similar car outside the school ...

Or had there?

Somewhere behind, a man was running. A voice shouting. There seemed to be something urgent in the sound. Nicky glanced behind him and saw a distant, track-suited figure pacing along the pavement. The new teacher.

'Catch the ball!'

His attention was jerked back to the issue at hand as the tennis ball bounced up in front of him, hitting him in the face. Lou laughed loudly and derisively as Nick faltered in his step, madly clutching for the ball. It bounced away and he chased it, and a moment later he bumped into the dark, smelly shape of a tramp.

The man had picked up the ball, and peered down at Nick through dark-rimmed, bleary eyes. The man smelled awful, and he reached for Nick quickly, but the boy snatched the ball from his hand and raced away, heart pounding.

When he looked back a moment later, the dishevelled old tramp was walking after him. 'Run!' he yelled to Lou, and the two boys, acting as if they were being pursued by the evil agents of an alien warlord, fairly streaked along the road.

Nicky was half aware of the Mercedes that approached them, and a moment later he screeched his warning to Lou, watching frozen, and horrified, as the great car drove up onto the pavement and bore down upon them.

Running ... the sound of shouting ...

The silver car shooting towards him ...

His legs immobile, panic locking his limbs, so that he stood watching, helplessly, pathetically ...

A moment later he felt himself picked up and flung against the wall. He tumbled to the pavement, feeling Lou Hanvey's shaking body below his. The car roared past, then continued out of sight.

The new teacher – Mister Bodie – towered above him, peering down, breathing hard. Then he smiled. 'Enough exercise for a month. You boys all right?'

And swallowing hard, still dazed from being flung out of the car's pathway, Nick Stone nodded and said, 'Yes sir. Thank you sir.'

From a position, parked a few yards down the road from the Stones' house, Bodie watched as Anne Hanvey finally delivered Nick to the house. It had been a worried re-union, at the school, but Bodie had reassured the woman. He watched as Anne stood outside the house, telling Chrissie of what had happened, and he didn't like the clear signs of distress that he could see on Chrissie Stone's pale features.

Opposite the house, watching from the first floor of Mrs Aldiss's – the Stones' eccentric, over-imaginative neighbour – a CI5 agent called Monteith was a shadowy shape behind net curtaining. Bodie began to drive slowly past both houses, using his transmitter to speak to the surveillance man. 'That's one home safe and sound, six-two. Anything to report?'

Monteith's deep voice came back at him from the hand set, 'Quiet as the grave, three seven.'

'I'll let that pass,' said Bodie solemnly. 'Out.' He contacted Control again. 'Three seven. Patch me through to nine one, would you?'

A moment later Liz Spalding's slightly irritated tones spoke quickly into the receiver. 'You'll pay for this, three seven. You'll pay very dearly.'

'Kept late, eh?'

'Linda's detained for a while. Bad marks in Home Economics. Dammit.'

Bodie grinned. 'Screwed up the rice pudding?'

'Not half as much as I'd like to – ' the voice stopped. A moment later, in more controlled manner. 'Affirmative.'

'Well *stick* with her – all the way home.'

'Very funny, three seven. Out.'

The first day! They'd struck on the very first day. And no doubt they would strike again tomorrow, and the day after that. Now that they had made their first move, their first *real* move, they would not give up until Jack Stone did what he was supposed to do: start talking. Start remembering.

He stood at the side of his son's darkened room, watching Chrissie stroking the boy's forehead. Nick was asleep, but restlessly so.

'He's still a bit hot.'

Jack stepped forward and touched the boy's face. His temperature was high, almost feverish. 'Yeah. But he'll be all right. He's a bit shaken, a bit upset. He'll soon forget all about it. Come on down.'

Chrissie rose from beside the bed, and took Jack's hand as

they walked to the stairs. Jack squeezed his wife's cold fingers affectionately. He wished he really believed his own supportive words.

They were half way down the stairs when Linda came out of her room and called to him. 'Dad?'

'Yes love?' He looked back up at her and smiled. Chrissie went on down to the kitchen to make some tea. Jack walked back up to the landing and put his arm around his daughter. She was still wearing her school uniform and her socks were round her ankles. 'What is it, Lyn?'

She stared at him, her childish face at first impassive, then progressively emotional as she sought the words, trying not to cry. 'Was it ... was it an accident?'

'Almost certainly,' Jack said. 'Poor little thing, must have gone out through the cat door. Car got out of control. Some madman going too fast ... '

'But he never went out on his own. He was such a little dog. He always slept up here ... '

'I know love, I know. I can't tell you why he did it. All I know is that when I went out this morning I found the poor little thing, run over. I'll make it up to you.'

Linda was not to be placated. 'First Suki, now Squidge. I can't believe it, daddy. Does somebody hate us? I bet they deliberately ran Squidge over.'

Jack reached out to hug the girl. 'You're a big girl, now, Lyn, so I'll tell you that you're right. Someone round here doesn't like pets ... They make a mess, root up plants, flowers. There's some funny people about. We'll find who did it, love. And there'll be a new Squidge in the family before you know it.'

Linda pulled back from him, as he crouched beside her. She stared him full in the eye, as if seeking the truth in the way he looked at her, rather than in the words he spoke. 'Are you going to stay with us now? Will you be going away again?'

'No. I'm not going away again. Not right now. I'll be with you as long as I can ... '

'So you *will* have to go away again? Why can't you just stay home forever, daddy? Why do you have to go?'

'It won't be for long, love. And it won't be for a while. It depends on some friends of mine. Now get to bed, and I'll see you in the morning.'

She kissed him on the cheek, then turned and went back to her room. Jack walked downstairs and went to the kitchen. Chrissie was standing by the stove, watching the kettle boil. As he came into the room, he realised that she was crying quietly, and he went up to her and put his arms around her as tightly and as reassuringly as possible.

## *Chapter Four*

Early the next morning, Ray Doyle watched impatiently in the computer room as information on the rest of the bank job team, which Jack Stone had led, was printed out into George Cowley's waiting hands. Cowley's meeting with the Commissioner had been successful: CI5 were fully invested with the authority to both guard Stone's family, and seek out the nature of the person or persons unknown who were harassing that family.

The print-out machine was suddenly silent. Doyle drew his restless gaze from the banks of silent consoles, and the rows of operators, many of them girls hardly out of school, and watched Cowley tear the sheet off and finish his cursory read of the contents.

'Nice day out for you, Doyle.'

'Oh yes, sir? Where's that, then?'

'Spot of prison visiting – Parkhurst, Isle of Wight, and Winchester ... ' He looked up at Doyle, rugged features implacable, and handed the sheet across. 'A simple day's work, for a man like you.'

'Who's on the island?' said Doyle, finding it difficult to interpret the densely packed information on the print-out sheet. He finally spotted the name, just as Cowley said, 'Barney Moss. It was he who put the job together and picked the team.'

'Yeah,' said Doyle. 'I remember him. A bit of a handful.'

'That's why he's in Top Security,' said Cowley, with a thin smile. Doyle tried to ignore him.

'Who's the one in Winchester?'

'That's Ned Turner, the draftsman. He didn't go on the job but did most of the planning. Then he rushed in for his money, a little too quick off the mark ... '

Doyle grinned. 'Perhaps he was worried about inflation.'

'Now he gets paid in sweets and tobacco.' Cowley chuckled as he made the point. He had had a personal hand in the arrest of Ned Turner.

Folding the sheet of paper into four, and slipping it in the back pocket of his denims, Doyle asked one last thing. 'Any news on the Mercedes?'

They walked towards the exit from the computer room. 'Regrettably not,' Cowley said. 'Bodie was wrong-footed. Can't blame him, the kids' lives were of paramount importance, and by the time he'd calmed them down, the car was well away.'

'No doubt that it would have killed Nick Stone, though?'

Cowley allowed that slight grimace of disgust to touch his face that told of his total contempt for this particular villain. 'No doubt at all. And not just the Stone boy. They would have sacrificed young Hanvey as well.'

Doyle drove straight to the Isle of Wight, arriving in time for the eleven-thirty ferry. Once on the island he lost no time getting to the prison, and within the hour was waiting in the ante-chamber to an interview room, listening to the distant, hollow sound of metal ringing on metal, and footsteps echoing morbidly as men exercised and moved about their token business.

He hated prisons, even the so-called modern set-ups where the relations between prisoner and prison-officer were the best that could be hoped for, and violence was minimal. Men in cages was not right. In Doyle's experience it rarely helped to develop the human side of the 'rehabilitated' man. He had spent time 'inside' himself, once, when an assignment that had taken him abroad had gone badly wrong. The heat, the insects, and the debilitating claustrophobia of those few terrifying days often returned to haunt him.

Men in cages. It made him long for the open fields of the island, again. He would be glad to get the interview done.

He watched as a prison officer led a squat, muscular, aggressive looking man into the interview room and sat him down. Barney Moss stared at Doyle through the intervening glass-topped door, and Doyle felt the hostility like tiny knives. Moss was in his early forties, but already looked ten years older than that.

When Doyle was finally conducted through, and seated across the table from the lag, Moss said gruffly, 'Well?'

'Very well, thanks,' Doyle retorted quickly. He drew out a pack of five cigars and tossed them towards Moss. 'I hope I find you the same.'

Moss grinned sourly. 'Yeah, it's great here. The sea air, the sun-drenched beaches.' He didn't take his eyes from Doyle, nor reach for the cigars.

Doyle nodded towards the pack. 'You were always a cigar man, weren't you Barney? Big cigar, big flash ... '

Moss picked up the packet, opened it, put four cigars into his pocket and stuck the other between his lips. 'Didn't bring a bird, I suppose.'

Quick as a flash, Doyle said, 'Piece of chicken? Could have, if I'd thought ... '

But Barney Moss didn't like the joke, stared at Doyle as if Doyle were the pits of the earth. After a second he said, 'So who the hell are you? A circus clown? What d'you want?'

'Ray Doyle. CI5. Information. From you. I want.'

Moss frowned, thinking hard. 'CI5 ... yeah, I know about them. But your name's familiar. Yeah, that's it. Doyle. You were in the regular force – Limehouse, wasn't it?'

Impressed with Moss's memory, Doyle nodded his head slowly. 'Sure. Did a bit there. Did a bit all over.'

'And now you're in the "Derring-do Mob". Dirty tricks. Beyond the law. I hope you get well paid for it.'

'It's a living.'

'So's keeping pigs,' observed Moss evenly. Doyle realised that there was just the hint of a smell of animal about the man. So that's what Moss did now. Master of the sty. Moss repeated, 'So what's it about?'

'The Maiden Lane job. Bank of America.'

'Oh no! Not again.' Moss took the unlit cigar from his mouth, reached across the table for Doyle's lighter. As he puffed the cigar to life, he shook his head, a man weary of going over the same ground again. 'Listen. There's a book on it, right? And another one coming out. And that TV presenter chap has analysed us psychologically, and one of the Sunday's is serialising the new book, and there's some women's rag did the female angle, and enough's enough. You could always read the trial transcripts. Six weeks, plus the appeals. Should take you to Christmas.' He leaned back, savouring the cigar, letting the smoke drift slowly from between his slightly parted lips.

Ray Doyle waited a moment, meeting the arrogant gaze coolly. 'Read the book,' he said. 'Thought it stank. Checked the trial transcripts too ... '

'Thorough boy. What d'you need me for?'

'One question was never answered. None of you answered it. And I'm asking now: who put up the seed money? Who wanted the job done in the first place?'

Barney Moss grinned, then winked at Doyle. 'Well, Mister Doyle. Now you're asking. Now you're really asking ... '

It didn't take Ray Doyle more than a minute to realise that he was backing a loser. He repeated his question, and came up against the same smiling ignorance. Barney Moss either didn't know *who* had staked the seed money ... or he wasn't telling, and not even the Spanish Inquisition was going to change that state of affairs.

So Doyle got the ferry back to the mainland and drove quickly to the attractive, still-recognisably medieval city of Winchester. He had never visited the prison here before, and it took him a while to find it. But by late afternoon he was waiting in the exercise yard as the tall, rather lean shape of Ned Turner stepped out to join him.

Turner squinted against the sudden brightness. His face was sallow, his lips curled down in a perpetual sulk. He saw Ray Doyle, glanced back at the prison officer, who nodded: he's the one.

'Doyle?'

'The very same.'

'What're we doing out here?'

They began a slow walk around the exercise yard, Turner rubbing his eyes, slightly distracted by the daylight. Doyle could see bruises on the man's neck. Turner wasn't a naturally violent man, and Doyle guessed that he had been 'put upon' inside, and had probably objected.

'This is a bonus,' said Doyle. 'A bit of fresh air.'

Cynically, Turner said, 'Acclimatising me, are you? For Open Prison?'

'Bit soon for that, Ned. Still, a word in the right direction ... '

Turner was suspicious of the other man, as he quite rightly should have been; but he'd had a whiff of something he especially didn't like, which considering who and what Ray Doyle was, was an amazing mistake to make. 'You some sort of God Botherer? Come to rescue my soul?'

Doyle was taken aback, and looked slightly morose as they paced around the yard. 'I shall have to start taking the "hard tablets" again. God Botherer indeed! Er, no. No I'm not. You could say I'm a Concerned Person.'

'Concerned about what?' They were passing the silently watching prison warder again. Turner ignored the man with a calculated deliberateness.

Doyle said, 'Jack Stone's wife and kids.'

Turner immediately stopped dead in his tracks, gave Doyle a look that might have killed. 'Don't tell me you're collecting.'

'In a way,' said Doyle evenly, meeting the hard stare until Turner's gaze broke away.

'Insurance?'

'Not exactly,' said Doyle. 'Someone's threatened to exterminate them.'

Whatever reaction Doyle had expected, he hadn't expected a sneering laugh. Turner shook his head. 'Chrissie and the kids? No way. Not while her father's alive, not while the Hatchet can still cut it.'

'It does seem a bit extreme,' Doyle agreed, 'but if it was only a rumour I wouldn't be here. It's definitely on. The boy was nearly killed yesterday ... '

Turner looked quickly at Doyle, and there was worry on

his face. It was clear that he was increasingly suspicious of his visitor, especially now that the talk had turned to 'vengeance'. 'What mob are you, then?' Doyle flashed his CI5 ID card. Turner took one look and groaned. 'I think I'll go back inside.'

'Not chilly, are you?' said Doyle teasingly. 'It's nice out here.'

'Yeah. On a clear day you can see the Cathedral.' Turner had faced back towards the exit from the yard, but he hesitated, saying, 'I know what your game is, Doyle. Carrot and Stick. You're the Carrot and I don't want to meet the other fellah. Get my meaning?'

Placatingly, and with a boyish smile, Doyle assured the lag that he had left his 'Stick' back at Control. 'You've always been marked down as the non-violent type. You wouldn't want the Stone family harmed, now, would you?'

'Not them,' said Turner grudgingly. 'But I could do him a bit of harm. Stone. The queue forms on the right.'

'The queue?'

'Come on!' said Turner irritably. 'He rung it on us, all of us. Jack Stone! I could do with an hour alone with him!'

Doyle could understand the feelings that bubbled up in Ned Turner, the grudge, the anger, the frustration. 'Rings you up. Gets clean away. Don't seem fair ... '

Turner sneered. 'No. It doesn't seem *fair*. Colin died. You knew that, did you? Car burnt out when it turned over. He was Chrissie's cousin. The Hatchet's nephew. Burned alive. *And* the rest. All sorts of things got burnt when that car went over. Jack got out, though. Jack Stone. Crawls from the wreckage. Never been seen since. Has he?'

Doyle shrugged. 'I wouldn't know. What's the word inside?'

But Turner wouldn't rise to *that*. He smiled thinly, let his narrowed eyes coolly appraise the hard-looking young man beside him. 'Oh Mister Doyle ... you should know better than that.' And he walked out of the yard.

After his second day as substitute games and sports master,

Bodie drove wearily to CI5, and checked in at Forensic, then at Traffic.

From both departments he received information that might help free the Stone family from harassment. He sought out George Cowley, and found the man waiting impatiently in the basement garage, watching as a mechanic worked below his car.

'Ah, Bodie,' Cowley said solemly, hardly taking his attention from the gleaming vehicle on its hydraulic ramp. 'How's the world of Lower Education?'

'Might take it up full time, sir,' said Bodie with a thin and slightly arrogant smile. 'Before I get too old for CI5.'

Cowley looked at him sharply. 'I hope that wasn't meant to be facetious, Bodie.'

'Who me sir? No sir. I just got this from Forensic. A nice twist on the note.'

Cowley frowned. 'What note would that be?'

'Jack Stone. The letter threat.' Cowley nodded quickly, remembering the crumpled piece of paper with the threat upon it. Bodie went on, 'Nothing in the way of prints, except Stone and his missus. Standard cheap writing paper – there's reams of it on sale, about four hundred outlets. But the lettering's done with the right hand by a *left handed* male, of medium height and weight, probably in his forties.'

There was an unmistakable hint of cynicism in Cowley's expression as these facts were reeled off, all deduced from a sample of scrawled writing. 'Now if he was dyslexic, or only had one leg. No hints as to that in the note, I suppose?'

''Fraid not, sir. It *would* narrow the field a bit, wouldn't it? But there's nothing wrong with the spelling, and no one said anything about limping as he wrote.'

'Put it through the computer anyway. Something's better than nothing.'

Bodie smiled. 'I already have. The left-handed are as crooked as the right handed, even when they're medium males. This might be more help.' He held out the second fact-sheet, and Cowley glanced down as Bodie said, 'A "K" registration Mercedes SL. It came in through Traffic.

Apparently the number plates don't tally with any registered for a Merc.'

'That's nice,' Cowley agreed, glancing back at his own car, which was now slowly descending on the ramp.

'Keep it under observation. Or bring it in?'

Cowley said, without pause, 'Observation. It's worth a few days observation.'

Bodie folded the paper. 'Anything from Doyle?'

'A wall of silence. He thinks that something is known, but they're not telling. He's seen Moss and Turner already. The rest of the gang during today and tomorrow, but I don't think he'll have much luck.'

'But they won't be able to get word out that he's been to see them.'

Opening the rear door of his car, Cowley climbed in. His chauffeur was already in place, and waiting. 'Not till it's all over,' Cowley said, looking out and up at Bodie. 'A touch of solitary. They'll be told why afterwards.'

He slammed the door closed, and the car drove smoothly away, and out into evening London. The young mechanic stood watching it go, wiping his oily hands on a rag.

Bodie said, 'Sounds a bit rough.' And smiled.

The mechanic scowled. 'Thanks a lot.'

Unaware that the first tightening tugs on the net around her family's attackers had begun, Chrissie Stone arrived back at the house at six that same evening, the boot of her small car loaded with supermarket supplies. She parked outside the garage and turned off the engine. As she went round to the boot she saw the furtive movement in one of Mrs Aldiss's bedroom windows. *Busybody*, she thought. It had not occurred to her that the snooping might have been on a more professional level.

She swung the boot cover up and reached inside for the two carrier bags of supplies. One had toppled over, and eight oranges had rolled and scattered about the small compartment. As she gathered them together, she noticed a small pamphlet stuffed inside the first carrier bag, and puzzled she pulled it out.

It was one of those religious pamphlets that occasionally get pushed through the letterbox, only to be instantly thrown away: The Watchtower. But she couldn't remember anyone approaching her, or giving her the document.

Almost disinterestedly, she turned the paper over, and gave a gasp of shock, her heart missing a beat.

A message had been scrawled there!

'One, Two . . . almost Three. Did he get the message? Did he *get* the message? One, Two, Poor little Three . . . '

She slammed the boot down, with a cry of 'God Almighty!' and ran indoors, where she sat down at the kitchen table and beat her fists against the wood, with anger, with frustration, with a sudden, desperate concern for Nick.

It was the longest night she had ever spent. Sleep was impossible, even though Jack shared her bed, that night, resigned to the fact that his whereabouts would be known soon enough. In the darkness, arms around each other, they came to a decision, and though the decision was a relief for Chrissie in terms of her two kids, it was a sad one for the two adults. It would have a consequence for Jack Stone that hardly bore thinking about.

Before dawn, Chrissie was up and making preparations. She had packed two cases with clothes, towels and essentials. She had found a large blanket, which she placed in the back of her car, in the garage. Then she roused the two children, urging them to be quiet, and to quickly wash, dress, and eat a bowl of cornflakes. They seemed confused as to what was going on, but were too sleepy to make too loud an objection.

When they had eaten breakfast, Jack ushered them into the garage, to the car, and pushed them onto the floor, behind the driver's seat. 'Get down!' he said, in hushed, urgent tones. 'Get down and stay down, until your mother says you can get up!'

'Daddy . . . what's going on?' Linda's confusion was bringing her close to tears. A sensitive child, she could tell that something was wrong with her father ... with everything.

Jack kissed them both, then covered their small bodies with the blanket. He hugged Chrissie for a moment or two.

'Hope we're doing the right thing,' he whispered.

Chrissie squeezed him tighter. 'It's all we can do, Jack. Thieves take care of their own ... ' she sounded bitter as she spoke that last.

Jack said, 'Leave it out.'

He kissed her quickly on the lips. She looked sad as she drew away from him. 'They'll come for you, now. Doyle ... that lot. They'll take you in.'

He motioned her to silence, then watched her climb into the car and start the engine. It purred gently. He went to the garage door and opened it as quietly as possible.

Remaining hidden as best he could, he glanced down the street both ways. It was deserted. He beckoned Chrissie out and she reversed down the drive and out onto the road.

A moment later she was gone, and the garage door was closed again. Jack went to the front window of the lounge and looked out between the net curtaining. He saw the indiscreet movement of the CI5 man across the road, and guessed that the man's attention had been distracted after the long night's watch, and he had missed the car's departure. Suddenly spotting the rear view of the vehicle, he had leaned out of the window, and was using his R/T to contact his base. Stone felt a moment's irritation, but with luck, and following the roundabout route that they had worked out the evening before, Chrissie should make any tail difficult to pick up on her.

She drove so frantically to begin with that it finally occurred to her that she was running the risk of being stopped for speeding. She had put four miles between the children and the house, and the roads were empty and easy. She could see no sign of anyone following her.

The children were hot. Nick was feeling cramped and claustrophobic, and kept peeking out from below the blanket until dragged back down by Linda.

'Do what daddy said! Stay down.'

'It won't be long,' Chrissie said from the front, reaching back to ruffle Nick's hair through the woolly covering.

She could see the motorway flyover up ahead, but would not take that faster route west just yet. Instead she drove along side roads, following the motorway in parallel, always watching her rear-view mirror.

The red saloon glided into view between one glance and the next.

'Oh no . . . '

She couldn't see who drove it, whether it was the familiar face of either Doyle or his companion, but it seemed to be keeping its distance. She turned to the right and the red saloon followed her round, a hundred yards behind.

It suddenly began to close the distance between them and Chrissie felt her heart beat increasing to an almost violent rate. Unconsciously, she stepped down on the accelerator and pulled ahead of the saloon again. She had to brake hard to avoid a milk-float that loomed ahead of her suddenly. She overtook it, and sped down a road to the left, getting back on the route that ran beside the motorway.

And with a sigh of relief she noticed the red car continue straight on along the road behind her.

'Won't be long, kids,' she said more confidently, and slowed for a roundabout, taking the second exit. 'Soon be able to come up for air.'

She put her foot down, impatient to join the motorway and get this journey over with. There was a trickle of traffic, now, and she overtook the sleepy drivers with an almost reckless haste. She drove through an area of shops, where already fruiterers were stacking their display boxes out on the pavement.

Nick poked his head up from the blanket and looked around. No harm now, Chrissie thought, and glanced back at her son with a reassuring smile.

When she looked back at the road, the red saloon was coming towards her. She felt instantly startled, slightly puzzled . . .

Then panic struck, as the red saloon veered towards her,

running along her side of the road, accelerating rapidly.

Head on collision!

'Oh my God!' she screeched, and spun the wheel, running the car up onto the pavement, twisting the wheel to try and avoid a shopkeeper, and plunging head-on into the wide, plate-glass window of an antique shop.

The last thing she heard, before blackness closed over her, was the violent, hysterical screaming of her two children.

Bodie received the message about the sneaky departure of Chrissie and the two children as he was jogging round the block, just after six in the morning. Doyle had already been told and was furious.

For a second Bodie was undecided as to what he could, and should, do now. No point in turning up at the school if young Nick wasn't going to be there.

He jogged easily back to his apartment, to snatch some breakfast, and was just passing his own car when Control made contact with him again through the bulky R/T he carried.

'She's smashed the car. Eastern Way. The police are there now.'

'Oh God. How are they?'

'Bruised, but alive. Four five's on his way.'

'Right.'

He drove rapidly to the scene of the accident. An ambulance was just pulling away, and since there was no sign of the Stone family, he guessed they were now en route to the nearest hospital.

Doyle was just climbing out of the shattered window of the junk shop. He looked haggard and angry as he walked over to his partner.

'What happened?' Bodie asked.

'On their way to the grandparents. Seems they didn't rate our efforts at protecting them ... '

Bodie glanced at the wreck of the Stones' car as it was slowly winched back across the pavement by the police breakdown truck. 'After this I'm inclined to agree. How'd they manage to slip away?'

Doyle looked disgusted. 'Our man took his eye off the ball. I gave him a rocket, but that was more for my own good than his. It could've happened to anybody. Crack of dawn after a long night ... made himself coffee and got back to the station as the car was disappearing from view. Lucky he spotted it at all.'

They stared at the wrecked car. Bodie said, 'What's the damage?'

'More shock than anything. Chrissie's got scratches and bruises. She had her belt on, thank God. Kids are just hysterical.'

Bodie scowled, angry at the way a family, which had asked for protection, could then make itself so vulnerable by not trusting the judgment of the men they had hired. 'Cowley's going to love this,' he said bitterly. 'We should have turned Jack Stone in in the first place and let the Met boys worry about protecting the family.'

Doyle glanced at his partner irritably. 'Well we didn't, did we? And it's on our shoulders.' He looked one last time at the car, as it was winched onto the trailer. 'And I want this mad bastard. I want him bad ... '

## *Chapter Five*

Shortly after eleven, on that same morning, George Cowley arrived at the neatly maintained country house that belonged to Len Hatch, Chrissie's father, and a man more familiarly known in Cowley's circuit as The Hatchet.

Cowley was met at the front door by an elderly, but still handsome woman, dressed in trouser suit and a very westernised poncho. This was Rosalind Hatch – Roz – and she greeted Cowley coolly, but courteously, before leading him through the house and into the rear garden.

Len Hatch was in his long greenhouse. Cowley followed Roz across the garden, making conversational comment upon the neatness of the flower borders, and the obvious care that had gone into making the garden a comfortable and relaxing place for both adults and children.

'Hatch! Someone to see you.'

She led the way into the greenhouse, commenting, 'He doesn't like the name Len. I always call him Hatch.'

Len Hatch looked up from the tall tomato plants that he was tending, then looked back to what he was doing. He was a trim looking man in his early sixties, dressed in casual, but tasteful clothes, and wearing a pair of gold-rimmed half-glasses. At first glance, Cowley thought, he looked like a retired accountant.

But as Hatch stared at Cowley, as the men came close, Cowley could see that there was a more dangerous quality in the man's cool gaze, and in the cut of his jaw. Despite his age, Len Hatch was still a man to be reckoned with.

The Hatchet had not lost those qualities which had made him one of the most respected, and feared, members of the underworld.

'Good morning,' said Cowley pleasantly, and then introduced himself, and his department.

Hatch considered him carefully, not bothering to look at the ID card that Cowley had held out for inspection. 'Good morning to you.' He glanced at Roz. 'Coffee on? I could do with a cup. I'm sure Mister Cowley could do with a cup too.' It was part question and Cowley smiled, and indicated affirmatively to the woman.

Clearly dismissed, she left the greenhouse. Hatch bent down to the plants. He was tying the fragile stems to canes for extra support as the plants grew tall.

'Is this how you put in your time now?' said Cowley.

'It's better than the other way.'

'Yes. I expect it is. You seem to be very comfortably placed. A very nice house, nice grounds.'

Hatch glanced up suspiciously. 'All bought and paid for. You want to see my accounts?'

Cowley smiled and shook his head. 'No thank you, Hatch. I'm sure they make tight, well-plotted reading.' Hatch snickered, a touch of humour, responding well to Cowley's cool cynicism. Cowley said, 'We've met before.'

'Have we? Can't say as I remember.'

'Presentation dinner for Jimmy Dix, back in '72.'

Hatch looked up quickly, nodded slightly. 'I was there. Don't remember seeing you. It was well attended ... '

'It was certainly well attended. A few months later the Corruption Trials began.'

'Jimmy did his time,' Hatch observed quietly. 'Stood it well. He's in South Africa, now. Security Man in the gold mines. Right place for him!'

'Indeed,' said Cowley, wryly. 'I want to talk to you about Maiden Lane.'

Hatch straightened up from the plant box, and surveyed his handiwork for a second before looking at Cowley and saying, 'Maiden Lane or Memory Lane? You come out with some ripe ones. Besides ... ' he picked up an apple box of small shrubs and pushed past Cowley, along the damp walkway of the greenhouse. 'I had nothing to do with it.'

'No. But your son-in-law did. That's why I'm here, Hatch, because of him, because of your daughter and grandkids.'

Hatch looked up sharply as he placed the box of shrubs on the side. 'What are they to do with anything? Jack had it away at the time. More luck than brains . . .'

'*Did* he have it away, Hatch? Is that true?'

Hatch sneered. 'Half the world's police *and* Interpol never got near him. Maybe he did have a bit of something – cunning, animal cunning. Maybe.'

'Who supports his family?'

'Who d'you think? I do, of course. The bastard never left her a thing. Dropped her right in it. Worthless slob.'

'Who else do you know who thinks Jack Stone is a worthless slob?'

'Quite a few, I'd have said.' Hatch frowned, suspicious of the sudden direction of questioning. Before Cowley could add anything further, Roz Hatch appeared on the back lawn, carrying a tray of coffee, which she placed on the wide garden table. Hatch led the way from the greenhouse.

'This is very kind of you, Mrs Hatch,' Cowley said.

'No trouble,' she answered, and with a glance at her husband added, 'I won't join you, if you'll excuse me. My daughter's bringing the children over and I've a lot to do.'

Quickly, Cowley said, 'I don't think they *will* be coming, Mrs Hatch. Not just yet.'

Roz Hatch looked startled; Hatch's eyes widened behind his glasses, then he frowned angrily. 'How's that? What d'you mean, they won't be coming?'

As calmly as possible, Cowley told them about the accident on the outskirts of London.

Roz said, 'Oh my God,' covering her mouth with her hand.

'Accident! My daughter, my grandkids hurt, and you've been quizzing me about some job years ago that didn't even involve me!'

'Don't distress yourselves,' Cowley said evenly. 'They're all right. Your daughter has bruising and some scratches. Your grandchildren are unhurt, just a little shocked. And the accident and that job, years ago though it was, are related.'

Roz Hatch looked very distressed. 'Where are they? Tell us where they are!'

'They're being taken care of. They're quite safe.'

Hatch snapped, 'Well, I want to see them!'

Trying to keep a note of authority in his voice, Cowley said firmly, 'You will. You both will. All in good time. Now – who hates your son-in-law enough to kill off his wife and kids?'

That was too much for Roz. She sat down heavily on one of the garden chairs, shaking her head in shock. 'Kill them ... oh God no. Not that.'

Her husband watched her, concerned for her, for his family. He was looking thoughtful and puzzled when he met Cowley's gaze again. 'Kill them, eh? Someone's had a go at them, that what you're saying?'

'Yes I am. Two attempts, both involving cars. Whoever it is made a start with the cat and dog, the family pets.'

Hatch shrugged. 'The cat was poisoned, I'd thought. Some neighbour didn't like it. Nutcase.'

'The cat was ripped open. It wasn't a neighbour. The puppy, too. Poisoned first. A very vicious killing.'

'Chrissie didn't tell us about that,' said Hatch quietly. 'It was us who gave the kids the dog.'

'What *did* Chrissie tell you? About why she wanted to bring the children over.'

'Just that she wanted to be on her own for a bit.'

Roz added, 'She gets depressed. It gets on top of her, Jack missing and all. She's brought the kids here before, give herself a bit of freedom.'

Cowley realised that he had to tread very carefully with a wily old bird like Hatch. He didn't want to risk letting Hatch know that Jack Stone was back in circulation. Hatch might have put his daughter's interests first, and decided that Stone was better off out of things, and two vengeance trails might be too complex for CI5 to handle thoroughly. He said, 'Would Chrissie tell you if she *did* hear from Jack?'

'She'd tell me,' said Hatch carefully. 'Of course she would.' The phone in the house started to ring. Roz got up to answer it, and when she'd vanished into the lounge,

Hatch added, 'Jack'll never show. He's not that stupid. You'll never find him now.'

'He must miss his family,' Cowley observed.

Hatch laughed derisively. 'Miss his family! He's probably shacked up with some bint somewhere. That's about the only good thing that came out of that bank job! Chrissie got rid of him. Oh, she misses him, yes, but she's better off without him, and she'll see the truth of that before too long. She needs to settle again, find a nice, regular bloke.'

'Is she looking?'

Hatch shook his head, shrugged in an almost despairing way. 'Women! They make no sense, half the time.'

Then Roz Hatch appeared on the patio, and called to Cowley. The phone call was for him. Someone called Doyle.

The hospital had finished with Chrissie Stone in less than two hours. Her cuts were treated, her bruises examined, and then she and the two children sat in the lounge of one of the private wards, sipping tea and waiting for Bodie to come and pick them up. When Bodie arrived he was in the company of a female operative whom he introduced as Liz Spalding.

Linda recognised her from the previous day at school. The new teacher! Liz just winked at the girl. 'We get around, we part-time teachers.'

Bodie noticed quickly that Liz and Linda had a rapport going, the child quite impressed, quite in awe of the older woman. That was good, he thought. With Chrissie so shaken up, it would be good to have a second voice in the Stones' house that could exert some control over the eleven-year-old. Nick just seemed subdued, rather pale, still quite shocked by the crash.

Briefly Bodie explained what was going to happen: that Liz was going to be smuggled into the house from the taxi that would take the family home, and she was there just to be on the safe side, in case the man who had killed their two pets came back late at night. She was a policewoman of sorts, and would arrest him on the spot.

Was that clear?

Nick and Linda nodded their heads, Nick morosely,

Linda obviously quite excited at this new turn of events.

They trooped down to the hospital's underground parking lot, and there Chrissie and the children took their places in the back of the black London cab that would be driven by Bodie. Liz Spalding squatted down on the floor, winked at Nick, then covered herself with a blanket. 'Don't look at me,' she whispered. 'Just pretend I'm not here.'

Bodie drove quickly to the Stones' house, slowing down as he came into the street at the far end. 'Coming up to it now. OK Liz?'

'Still here,' the woman said from the rear seat floor.

'OK, Chrissie?'

Chrissie nodded glumly, her bruised and scratched face peering sadly at Bodie, a small reflection in his rear-view mirror.

'Don't forget Linda – you go and open the garage while your mother pays me off. Make a thing about getting your bike out. All set?'

'All set,' said the girl. 'Then mummy tells me I can't go out and I'll wheel the bike back into the garage.'

'That's it,' said Bodie with a smile over his shoulder at her. 'Bit of a fuss, bit of distraction, and the lovely Liz gets into the house unseen. OK, Nick?'

The boy pouted slightly, but nodded his head.

Bodie slid the taxi into the kerb and stopped. Linda jumped out and went the few paces to the garage, unlocking the door and sliding it part way open. Chrissie climbed out of the cab, with Nick, and as they stood on the pavement so Liz Spalding slipped out of the taxi between them, bent low, and darted into the garage. Linda appeared with her bicycle, and reluctantly returned it to the gloom of the garage when Chrissie called to her to do so.

The whole operation had taken a few seconds only, a little huddle of activity in all of which the discreet entry of Liz Spalding to the house had had a good chance of going unnoticed by any distant, watching eyes.

As Bodie took off in the cab, he flicked on his R/T and contacted Monteith, on watch again from across the road. 'All quiet?'

'All quiet,' came Monteith's voice. 'Nicely done, three seven. Very nicely done.'

'Stick with it,' said Bodie. 'The night man cocked up.'

'So I heard. So I heard.'

Cowley took the phone from Roz Hatch as she picked it up and passed it to him, then left him to his privacy.

'What's up Doyle?'

'Just a progress report sir. The car that forced Chrissie Stone off the road was dumped outside the Underground station, less than half a mile away from the crash.'

'How'd we get the identity?'

Doyle said, 'A kid was delivering papers. He saw the whole thing, told the local division.'

'Gold star community service,' Cowley muttered. Most kids these days would have enjoyed the spectacle, told their mates, and never thought about reporting the events to the local police. Who'd want to get involved with the Fuzz?

'Anything on the licence plates?' he asked Doyle.

'Stolen last night, from North West Ten. The owner didn't even know it had gone.'

'Some careless people about.'

'Yeah. Can he have it back?'

'If we're finished with it, why not?'

He placed the receiver down, stared at it thoughtfully for a moment, then turned back into the room, intending to join the Hatches in the garden.

He was quite surprised to find Roz Hatch in the room with him. She was standing by the fireplace, staring at the photographs that were crowded along the mantlepiece top. If she had been listening she wouldn't have learned much from the brief courtesy call from CI5 HQ.

Cowley walked across to her and she looked up and smiled. Hatch was still in the garden. Cowley could see him sitting at the garden table, staring blankly into the distance. 'The Family in happier times,' Cowley observed, picking up a wedding photograph which he knew to be of the Hatches' daughter and Jack Stone.

Roz seemed slightly disconcerted, but she said, 'Yes.

Happier times is right. Hatch said it: Jack Stone was the worst thing that could have happened to Chrissie.' She picked up another photograph, this one clearly the work of an amateur. 'This is Chrissie seven years ago, at Nick's christening. She looks happy there.'

Cowley took the picture and smiled as he peered at it. 'Aye. He's a bonnie little lad.'

'Here he is again as a page at Col's wedding. Hatch likes to take photographs, and I think Nick is his favourite. We've got more of that lad than we have of Chrissie.'

Again Cowley took the picture, and smiled; but his mind was racing, searching for the link between what Roz had said and the image he held of a man, killed in a car crash. The picture was signed: 'Colin and Peggy, love to Roz and Hatch'. Cowley said aloud, 'Barely a toddler even then. Sweet little lad. Who's the couple? Colin? That wouldn't be Colly Roberts – killed when the getaway car burned out?'

Roz nodded solemnly. She took the photograph back and sighed as she stared at it. 'Yes it would. Poor Col. He wasn't a bad boy, just easily led. That's Linda, standing beside Peggy. First time as bridesmaid. Her hair was much fairer then.' She placed the picture back on the fireplace, picked up a small, black and white print of the bride. 'One of Peggy on her own. Do you know that's the last picture we ever got of her? She went out of her mind, poor girl. I hardly knew her, but I wasn't surprised when she . . . well . . . did it; you know . . . '

'Took her own life?' prompted Cowley.

'An overdose. Poor kid.'

'And who's this?' Cowley picked up a photograph of a sombre looking man of about forty, his face registering all the discomfort he was probably feeling in wedding suit and stiff shirt.

'That's Pat, Pat Weaver. Peggy's Dad. He didn't mix much, and we don't hear anything of him these days. And here's The Group. Look at us, what a bunch. Father, me, all of them . . . ' Cowley looked at the family photograph. Roz Hatch had been a real looker in her time, and the family portrait said one thing to Cowley above all else: we stick together. We're Family!

'Got you looking at the Zoo Pictures, has she?' Hatch's voice from the french windows startled Cowley, and he looked around and smiled acknowledgement. 'She'll get the family albums out at the drop of a hat . . . '

Cowley smiled at Roz, reassuringly. 'And why not? I do the same myself. Pat Weaver,' he added, almost absently. 'There's a name from the past.'

Ignoring him, Hatch said, 'Coffee's gone cold. Just as well. I'm due for a drink. How about you Mister Cowley? Too early?'

'It's late enough. A small scotch, perhaps.' As Hatch moved to a small drinks trolley, well stocked with spirits, Cowley took a last, lingering look at the photograph of Patrick Weaver, father of the dead bride. To Hatch, he said, 'Colin Roberts was your nephew?'

'That's right.'

'No sons of your own?'

'No. Just Chrissie and her sister, out in Miami. How do you take your scotch? Water?'

'Exactly as God made it.' He accepted the glass and raised it slightly, savouring the aroma of the expensive blend that Hatch stocked. 'What happened to the girl's father? Pat Weaver?'

Hatch sipped his own drink. There was something on his mind, anxiety, certainly, anxiety for his family; perhaps he had realised that if he was to get anything out of Cowley at all he was going to have to be co-operative. He shrugged. 'Weaver? Not a lot. Retired villain, not very highly thought of. He has a lot of time on his hands. Just like me. Time to think.' He took another sip of his drink, eyeing Cowley carefully. 'Come clean with me, Mister Cowley. This accident . . . it was to get at Jack, right? Jack Stone. He's back. Tell me I'm right, for God's sake. He's back, and someone's out for his blood. And Chrissie and the kids are in the line of fire.'

Cowley placed his glass upon the table, and pushed his

hands into his pockets, walking to the french windows and staring down the garden. 'Are you prepared to co-operate with us, in order to save the lives of your family?'

'Of course I am,' said Hatch angrily. 'We both are!'

Cowley turned to face him. 'Then I'll tell you what's going on, Mister Hatch. And the first thing you need to know ... ' he hesitated just briefly before saying it. 'Yes. Jack Stone is back. He's back with your daughter.'

Doyle made his way through the crowded, smoky billiard hall, towards the bar at the end, where he could see Bodie nonchalantly sipping a coke. It was the time of day when the tables were mostly occupied by kids, all dressed to the nines, playing more with the Steve Davis 'cool' than the Steve Davis 'skill'. There was only one game of billiards itself in progress, every other table rattling to the scatter of the reds and colours of snooker.

Ray Doyle preferred pub pool, a sharp, quick game, at which he was the Master ... at least over Bodie.

Bodie acknowledged him at the bar. 'Coke?'

'No thanks. You got here fast.'

'Better driver ... '

'Like hell.' Doyle's attention was drawn by a youth, wearing suit and bow-tie, who called to him from an empty table. 'You playing?'

'No thanks.' He turned back to Bodie. 'The word's out. The name. It's a long shot, but Cowley's sixth sense usually hits the mark ... '

'And the punter?'

'Name of Pat Weaver. Here's his picture. Quiet type, but with a neat turn in grievous bodily harm. Retired some years back to grow vegetables on an allotment, and sit and stare out of the window.'

'Active sort, you mean ... '

'Just the horses. Likes his flutter. We've a list to get through, looking for him. You can drive.'

They walked briskly down the length of the hall, idly watching the snatched shots, and the confident strokes that sent the white ball flying from the table. 'Not much class here,' Doyle observed.

'Good golf, though.' And on the subject of Pat Weaver: 'No address for him?'

'Cowley checked with the Housing Authority. Weaver had a Council flat, but let it go three months back. No forwarding address.'

They pushed through the end doors, and trotted quickly down the stairs to Bodie's car. 'Unusual, isn't it? Getting rid of a flat? They're hard to come by ... '

'Right. It also means he's lost his allotment. The allotment wasn't far from Jack Stone's place ... '

'Could've spotted Jack going "walkabout", you mean.'

'Right.'

They checked five local betting shops. No one had even heard of Pat Weaver, let alone seen him. Which Doyle knew was not the case, but this was a tight community, tight as a drum; they looked after their own.

By the time the last race was running, there was little point in checking the bookies for a sign of their man. Bodie swung the car in a tight circle and drove quickly back to the area of London where the Stones lived. They made their way to the sloping bank of allotments, where Pat Weaver had been tenant of lot 18.

It wasn't immediately obvious which was Weaver's patch. Half the allotment gardens were overgrown, constrasting starkly with the well-turned, well-planned intermediate patches, with their net-coverings, labelled rows of shrubs, and gleaming cloches. There was a scattering of greenhouses on the site, a few more wooden sheds, and several pigeon coops. When Doyle located lot 18, and found it to be totally overgrown and neglected, there was a man working on a neighbouring patch, and Doyle smiled at him as he walked past. 'Nice day for it.'

The man stopped digging, rested on his fork for a moment. Sweat glistened on his face. He was an old man, weather-beaten and ruddy, a man content with the slow pace of his life, and one who gained clear enjoyment from keeping his patch of vegetables weeded and productive.

'It's always a nice day for gardening. Most of these patches are run by summer gardeners. Sun comes out, here they are, digging and planting. Useless telling them they've missed the season.'

Bodie nodded towards Weaver's patch. 'Someone's really let this lot go to seed.'

The man nodded thoughtfully. 'That's Pat Weaver's patch. Not seen him for months. Used to keep it lovely; very conscientious man. He's probably turned his toes up, or moved away. Can't think why nobody else has taken it over.'

He returned to his digging. Doyle called across to him, 'Where'd he live? This Mister Weaver?'

Suspiciously, 'Why?'

'How long does it take to get a patch here?'

The man looked thoughtful. 'Oh, a good couple of years. You have to get your name down on the list . . . '

'That's what I thought. I'm a keen gardener, and someone told me that Pat Weaver's patch wasn't being used. I thought if I could see him . . . '

That seemed to please the older man. He scratched his head for a moment, then inspected his nails. Looking into the distance, he pointed across the new estates, nearby. 'I *think* he said he was getting a small place in one of them High Rises. He used to have a Council flat, but I think he got out of that. You might try them blocks.'

'Thanks,' said Doyle.

'You'd better hurry. Main planting season's nearly over.'

They struck lucky with the second block of flats. Bodie had talked to the caretaker of the first, and Doyle tackled the surly old man who resided in the basement apartment of the second. He liked to be called 'Sir', wore a patched black uniform jacket, probably a bus-conductor's jacket, and was quite unco-operative until Doyle identified himself.

Thereafter, the caretaker was his man, glad of a chance to finger 'that man' who had moved in with his girlfriend on the eighth floor. She, it turned out, was away, and had been away for some weeks, touring the clubs in the North. Some sort of singer cum comedienne, the caretaker thought. The man who shared her apartment was surly, unfriendly, and always complaining about the lifts and the garbage disposal.

Bodie listened to all this, outside in the car. He frowned at that last. 'You mean the lifts aren't working?'

'They are at the moment. Thank God. There's four fire doors per floor. That's thirty-two doors! No, if they're not working, we'll *make* them work.'

'Okay,' said Bodie, squinting up at the eighth floor. 'What's it going to be? Meter reader? I'll toss you for it.'

Doyle grinned. 'My turn with the flannel. It's Public Health Department. I'm conducting a survey on depressive tendencies in residents of high buildings.'

Bodie smirked as he climbed from the car. 'Oh yeah? Do you think you can keep up the patter?'

With a quick smile, Doyle said. 'But of course. I read *The Times*, don't I?'

They walked briskly into the block of flats and took the lift to the eighth floor. The landing was deserted as they stepped out, glancing quickly around. Bodie nodded towards the door of Flat 30 and Doyle stepped across to it, dropped to a crouch and peered in through the letterbox. 'I don't think there's anyone at home,' he said quietly, ringing the bell.

Bodie walked down the stairs, through one of the fire doors, a more discreet position from which to watch.

Doyle waited impatiently, ringing the bell a second time, watching his solemn-faced partner. Eventually he shrugged, drew out his skeleton-key pouch and began to work on the lock. Behind him, the lift shuddered and began to descend to the ground floor.

Smoothly, and swiftly, Ray Doyle gained illegal entry to the flat, gave Bodie a thumbs up, and vanished inside. He closed the door behind him, sniffing the air with distaste. Unopened windows, and stale food, combined to give a stuffy, unwholesome aroma to the place.

The flat was garishly decorated, the sort of expensive *chic* more commonly found in Chelsea. The cane furniture, silver framed pictures, and extravagant, wall-mounted lighting seemed out of place in this shoddy high rise. On the walls of the lounge were several photographs of the woman who owned the place. Doyle examined them quickly. She looked middle-aged, overdressed, a show-girl gone to seed.

Bodie contacted him on the R/T. 'All alone?'

'So far. No movement outside?'

'Lift's in use. That's all. No sweat.'

Doyle stepped through into the bedroom. The curtains were closed, the room stuffy with the smell of socks and sweat. The ashtray by the bed was crammed with cigarette butts, and two mugs of cold, scummy tea perched precariously on the bed-side table.

In the middle of the floor was a suitcase, opened, its contents of clothes ruffled and loose. Someone living, literally, out of a travelling bag, Doyle thought.

Bodie again, his voice a whispered murmur of urgency. 'Punter. Could be Weaver.'

'Got it,' said Doyle, equally softly. He moved quickly to the lounge, and stood behind the door, listening for the key to go in the latch.

But a moment later Bodie was on the channel again. 'False alarm. Relax ... '

'Okay ... ' Doyle went back to the bedroom and sorted through the case. At the bottom, wrapped in tissue paper, were two photographs, both showing the wedding of a young couple. From his earlier briefing, Doyle recognised the bride and groom as Col Roberts and Pat Weaver's daughter, Peggy. He called Bodie, 'He's been here all right. A whole flat to use, and he's lived in one room. Like a pig sty.'

'Find anything?'

'Not yet.' Doyle went through the pockets of the two pairs of slacks in the suitcase, but they were empty. He searched the rest of the flat, the bathroom especially, removing the wooden panels that covered the pipes, and poking around in the cistern. He checked the kitchen, inspecting the cupboards, and underneath the drawers. Underneath the sink he found a large tin of rat poison. Very little had been used.

He was about to call Bodie when he noticed a small white writing pad in the opened kitchen drawer. The light from the kitchen window was showing up the faintest of impressions on the paper, and Doyle picked up the pad and examined it more closely.

After a moment he smiled. Weaver had practised his right-hand script before scrawling the first note to Jack Stone.

'Bodie?'

'Standing by. You got something?'

Doyle said, 'One, Two, Three, Four, what's rat poison doing on the eighth floor?'

'Maybe they use the lifts?'

'No way. The dog was poisoned first, wasn't it? The Stones' dog?'

'I think so. That all you got?'

Doyle looked at the pad, where the words One, Two, Three, Four and Five had been repeatedly written on the missing top sheet. 'No. There's an inadvertent message from Weaver himself. We only have one problem, now.'

Bodie sounded almost weary as he said, 'Right. Where the hell's Pat Weaver?'

## *Chapter Six*

As night fell, and Weaver did not return to the flat he was sharing, Bodie and Doyle ceased surveillance on the eighth floor and drove the short distance to the house where Liz Spalding was standing guard over the Stone family. They parked the car some way away, and moved to their stations, to begin the long wait.

It was Cowley who had earlier put into words the fact that was so hard to take. 'Weaver will strike tonight. There's no reason for him not to. And it'll be the boy this time.'

'Would he really go so far?' Doyle had asked. 'It's Stone he wants, really. The animals, yes, putting the frighteners on. But would a man like Weaver do more than threaten the kids?'

'Was it a mere threat when Bodie saved the boy's life?'

'He might have veered off ... we just don't *know*.'

Cowley narrowed his eyes and shook his head. 'But I *do* know, Doyle. I've met Weaver's type many times before. He's a bitter, twisted man. The *need* behind the attacks is not a need that can be satisfied. It's not as if there was a stash of notes that he could extort from Stone and take away with him. The man wants revenge, pure and simple, and he's working logically through the family, saving Stone until last. It'll be the boy next, and it'll happen tonight. There's no reasoning with Weaver. Remember that. When his daughter committed suicide, every ounce of blame was placed squarely on Stone's shoulders ... '

Bodie said, 'What I don't understand is why he didn't attack the family immediately his daughter died? Why wait so long?'

'Because it's Stone's suffering that he wants. He didn't know Jack Stone was back until he spotted him, probably while he was working on his allotment. Stone making one of his surreptitious sorties to the phone box, and Weaver would have followed him, realised the set-up, and begun to plan his attack. He wants the man he sees as responsible for Peggy's death to suffer as much as possible before he takes Stone out himself. So be alert, on your guard. We don't want any casualties when we entice Weaver into our neatly-set web.'

As Ray Doyle and Bodie were moving into position outside the Stones' house, that night, inside the playroom Liz Spalding was being resoundingly beaten at table football. She had finally cracked the ice with young Nick, and was now flexing and exercising muscles, as she madly twirled and twisted the rows of red-painted wooden men, that she had almost forgotten she had.

The ball scooted into her goal for the ninth time, and Nick whooped with delight. Linda looked up from her book on horses and smiled. Earlier, she had played scrabble with the CI5 agent, and only narrowly lost.

Liz Spalding was a hit with the children, which was important to her; if Weaver did not attack that night, then she might be a regular presence in the house over the next few days, and it was essential that she had the trust and co-operation of the kids as well as Jack and Chrissie Stone themselves.

Chrissie looked into the playroom, and smiled as she saw the activity at the table-football. 'Come on, Nick. Time for bed.'

'Just another five minutes,' Nick begged, not taking his eyes from the ball as he whacked it half way down the table.

'You've already had another five minutes. I know your tricks. Get to bed.'

Liz Spalding straightened from the table, smiling broadly as she stretched her aching back. 'I'll have to concede anyway. He's seven ahead. I can't possibly catch up.'

Nick guessed that the evening's fun was over. Enthusiastically he said, 'How long're you going to stay with us, Liz?'

'Oh, a day or two perhaps,' she said, bending to kiss him goodnight. The boy scampered off, well pleased, all his earlier anxiety and depression passed.

Liz flopped down into the battered armchair opposite Linda, and glanced around the untidy playroom. She could quite happily spend a few days here, just remembering her own childhood: the train set, the beautifully designed doll's house, the football game . . . it made her sad that she had no children of her own so that she could cling on to that childhood that she so often missed.

As she reached to her bag for a cigarette, she realised that Linda was watching her curiously. She smiled. The girl had something on her mind, and finally voiced it: 'Have you got a gun in there?' There was an edge of concern in the youngster's tone.

Liz held up her cigarettes and lighter. Linda persisted, 'But *have* you? Have you got a gun?'

'Powder-puff, lipstick, driving licence. I've got all sorts of things in my bag, love, all sorts of things.'

Linda was intelligent enough to recognise when a question was being dodged. After a moment she said, 'Are you going to take Dad in?'

Liz Spalding shook her head as she drew on her cigarette. 'No. Not me. Not my job.'

'He's not a bad man,' the girl said, and there was a slight tremble in her voice; she knew that things had gone wrong for her father, and that there would soon be a time of parting.

'He's your Dad, Linda. I know what that means to you, how you feel. But if he's done something wrong, then he has to stand trial sooner or later . . . '

The girl asked, 'How long will he have to go for?'

Shrugging her shoulders, but trying to look as if the answer was 'hardly any time at all', Liz said, 'However long it is, you'll be able to see him regularly. And your Dad won't be hiding any more. That'll make all the difference to him.'

The door to the playroom opened and Jack Stone appeared. He acknowledged Liz quickly, then lifted his daughter into his arms. 'Bed for you too, love – '

'Oh, Dad. I want to stay up and talk to Liz . . . '

Jack Stone smiled and hugged the girl tighter. 'Bed, I

said. It's been a long day. Be a good girl, now.'

Picking up her bag, Liz Spalding walked to the door, 'I'll give Chrissie a hand in the kitchen.'

'Yeah, thanks.'

As she left, the last thing she heard Linda say was, 'Dad, I'm so frightened. Nothing's going to happen is it?'

'Don't be frightened, love. It's going to be all right.'

Liz Spalding shivered slightly. She was instantly aware of the responsibilities that sat upon her shoulders. She hoped fervently that Jack Stone would not be proven wrong.

At eleven that evening, Jack Stone entered the kitchen where Chrissie was sitting, drinking coffee and quietly staring out of the window into the darkness. Liz Spalding was in the lounge reading.

Chrissie looked up and saw that Jack was wearing his jacket. She frowned slightly, and he raised a finger to his lips, closing the kitchen door to, so that their words would not be heard by the woman in the other room.

'I'm going out for a few minutes.'

'Oh Jack you can't!'

'I must, Chris. I need to make a few calls.' He walked to the back door and peered out into the blackness. The light from a neighbouring house was illuminating part of the garden, and he could see the spade, still stuck in the earth where he had buried the puppy. He thought he glimpsed the slight gleam of light on a man's belt, somewhere towards the bottom of the vegetable patch. Bodie was somewhere near, he knew that, stationed within running range of the house. There was a second agent out in the darkness, at the front of the house. Doyle was waiting in his car a block or so away.

'I love you, Chris,' he whispered, turning back into the kitchen. 'I love you very much. The kids too. Done it all wrong . . . all wrong . . . '

'No, Jack. Not all. It'll soon be over with, and we'll soon be together again. But why must you go out?'

He leaned down on the table, a hollow-faced man, the concern for his family, the tension over his impending arrest, etching itself clearly around his eyes and mouth.

Chrissie reached out to cover his hand with hers.

'If I'm going to go away, there are several things to do, to arrange. I can't support you from inside, but I know your father will continue to give you what you need. I've got to talk to him, though. It's essential.'

'Why?' she asked, shaking her head. 'My father doesn't want to know about you. It's me and his grandchildren he's concerned about.'

Stone shook his head. 'Can't have him think that, love. When I come out, it's you and me again, and he's going to have to hear it from me. And there's a couple of blokes I need to talk to, old mates who I can trust for a good turn, if and when I hear that you need it. See? I've got to make the arrangements, love. It's for my own peace of mind.'

Chrissie smiled, squeezed her husband's hand, and nodded. 'Okay Jack. You do what you must. What can I do?'

'Nothing. If Liz asks, I'm in bed for a while. I'll be no more than twenty minutes, thirty at most. I'll slip out by the garage, and over the next garden.'

'Won't they see you?'

'I think I know where they are. I watched them deploying. See you, love . . . ' he stooped to kiss her, then walked easily into the kitchen, away from clear view from the garden. He opened the connecting door to the garage and stepped quickly into the darkness, feeling his way around the car and to the sliding door, which he moved open a few inches, allowing himself to slip out into the night.

At a crouch, he scanned the nightscape. There was no sign of either an agent or a man watching or approaching the house. Moving the garage doors closed again, he scurried to the fence between neighbouring gardens, passed quickly into the darkness of the trees next door.

Within minutes he had reached the streets leading to the allotment gardens that he would skirt, to find the phone box he had been using all the time he had been in hiding. Once across the allotments he walked more openly, even though he kept a wary eye out behind him.

He had just reached the box when a man on a bicycle appeared at the far end of the street. Stone crept into the shadows of the booth until the cyclist, his eyes on the road, his face half hidden beneath a peaked cap, had passed.

When it was safe to do so, Stone entered the phone box and began to make his calls.

He hadn't recognised the ageing, twisted features of Pat Weaver, as the man on the bike had cycled lazily past.

Nor had the CI5 man who was trailing Stone . . .

Minutes before, as Stone had slipped surreptitiously from his house, his furtive movement had been picked up by Dan Monteith, stationed at the front of the house, concealed in a neighbouring garden. If Stone believed he had slipped quietly away to the phone box, he had underestimated – or forgotten – the pursuit abilities of CI5. Almost the moment he had started to slide the garage doors back, that silent, almost invisible motion had been spotted by Monteith, using night glasses.

'Your man's going "walkabout",' he called through to Doyle, who lurched upright in his car, frowned, then swore.

'Better stay with him, six two. I'll move in closer to cover the front of the house.'

'Got it.'

Doyle shook his head angrily as he stepped out into the night and buttoned up his jacket. What the hell was Jack Stone up to? Surely he wasn't taking advantage of CI5's trust in him, and making a dash for it at night? It would make things far worse for him when he was eventually brought up for trial. As he loped silently into his new position, Doyle wondered if Chrissie Stone knew what her husband was up to. Probably not, he thought. She had recognised that Jack's jail sentence would probably – with parole – be fairly short, a year or two maybe, and she was more than prepared to sit those years out, now, in return for normal family life.

Doyle crouched behind a hedge, a hundred yards from the house, in a position where he had a good view of the road in both directions.

A normal family life, he repeated to himself, and smiled almost wanly at the thought of something that seemed destined to elude him for several years to come.

But it had not eluded Jack Stone, and he had thought that Stone was as prepared to pay his time in prison, in order to return to that normality, as Chrissie was to pay her time in waiting for him.

Doyle called Bodie on his small R/T.

'Three seven,' came Bodie's cold, hushed tones.

'Four five. I'm in a new position, replacing six two. Our man's gone walkabout for reasons of his own. Any movement out back?'

'Quiet, and cold, as the grave. Come on Weaver, you bastard. My joints are freezing up.'

'Stay alert,' said Doyle with a grin, and flicked off contact before Bodie could sourly tell him what to do with his advice.

Doyle rose on his haunches and checked the road. A lone cat was padding almost invisibly along in the lee of a low wall. Its green eyes caught light for a moment as it peered up at Doyle, then it had raced away into the night, a sleek, dark shape, perturbed by the presence of furtive human life on its territory.

A different sort of light flickered in the distance, and Doyle crouched down, squinting as he sought for shape and identity in the night.

'We may be in business,' he radioed to Bodie. 'Stand by.'

The light was unsteady, flickering across the road, and was soon revealed as belonging to a bicycle. The man pedalled wearily past Doyle's station, breathing heavily. He carried a canvas haversack, strapped across his shoulder, and was shaking his head as he cycled, a man tired and fed-up with his night-shift, and longing to get home, and into the warm.

I know how you feel, Doyle thought. He watched the bicycle pass right by the Stones' house, the tail light a small, red glow that faded from view.

'False alarm,' he called to Bodie, who expressed disappointment. Doyle checked the road again, then with a last glance at the vanishing cyclist, prepared to settle back behind his hedge.

He frowned, puzzled for a second.

The cyclist was nowhere to be seen. He had been moving slowly, and the street was dark . . . but he should still have been in view . . . shouldn't he?

Had he gone into one of the other houses?

Doyle moved quickly along the gardens, crouching slightly, eyes keen for movement, heart beginning to pump.

He only *just* glimpsed the Stones' garage door sliding to a close, a quick, difficult movement to observe in the darkness, a slight changing of shadows that caught Doyle's eagle eyes.

'Correction,' he called through to Bodie. 'We're in business. He's in the garage. Stand by . . . '

Doyle moved further up the road, and glanced up at the bedroom windows. Then he called softly through to agent nine one inside, warning her of 'company'.

Up to you, Liz, he thought grimly. If Weaver had been watching as Liz Spalding had been smuggled into the house, then the element of surprise was lost.

And her work would be cut out for her.

As Liz called softly that she was standing by, Doyle moved quickly across the road, his gun drawn and ready. A shoot-out was to be avoided at all costs, and though Weaver was cetainly armed, the moment he was confronted with two heavy-duty thirty-eight calibres, the game would be up. Wouldn't it?

Doyle reached the garage and gently moved the sliding doors, to follow Weaver inside . . .

He had to stifle his gasp of annoyance as he found the door to be locked. Weaver had slipped the bolt from the inside!

In the event, it all happened so fast that even had Doyle slipped into the garage after Weaver, he would have been too late to prevent tragedy.

Liz Spalding crouched on the landing, thirty-eight calibre pistol held firmly in her right hand, left hand on the stair rail, ready to drag herself into a standing position the moment Weaver came into her sight.

She heard the connecting door from the garage open and

gently shut. Cocking her head she could hear Weaver's furtive movements about the kitchen. What the hell was he doing? Trying to find a light switch?

Liz quickly tugged the red house-coat she was wearing a little more fully around her shoulders. It was cool on the landing, and she was shaking slightly . . . with the night cold, of course. The robe was Chrissie's, and when Weaver saw her wearing it, from the dimly lit hallway he would almost certainly think it was Chrissie standing there. The gamble was that Weaver was after the child, and would be so fixed on getting Nick that he would hesitate before letting off a shot at the woman.

A moment later the shadowy figure came into the hallway, hesitated for a second, then moved across to the stairs. By the thin moonlight that filtered in through the frosted glass on the front door, Liz could see that he held a silenced gun, and that its calibre was high.

Weaver had taken no more than one step upwards before she rose quickly to her feet, both hands holding her own pistol, and shouted, 'Here I am Pat. Drop the gun!'

Weaver cried out in shock, backing down the stairs, staring open-mouthed at the figure above him.

Then he raised his silenced gun and pointed it upwards.

'Drop the gun!' screamed Liz Spalding, her body dropping slightly to a crouch, the gun she held coming instinctively up to the fire position . . .

*He's going to shoot!*

In his panic, in the way his hand shook, in the gleam of madness in his eyes, in his silence . . .

It was all there . . .

*He's going to shoot!*

The silenced shot exploded upwards towards Liz Spalding as her own shot thundered through the house. The two children started to scream from the bedroom beside her. The glass lampshade in the hallway rattled with the shock of the report.

Liz felt herself thrown backwards, a numbing sensation in her right shoulder, her body totally weak. She stared at the floor, at the sudden crack of light beneath the bedroom door. She felt a sudden burning in her body, and a smell, like fresh meat, a choking, unpleasant smell.

She closed her eyes as blackness welled up to overtake her. It was too late, now, too late to help.

With a cry of pain, Pat Weaver lurched back into the kitchen, snatching his silenced gun from his dangling, useless left hand, holding it unsteadily in his right. He whimpered with the pain of the bullet wound in his shoulder. He thanked God it was dark so that he couldn't see the torn flesh, the ragged pit where the woman's shot had entered his body.

He flung the kitchen door open and staggered blindly out into the back garden, weaving his way across the lawn.

A man stepped out of the distant trees, braced his legs apart, hunched slightly and pointed a pistol at him.

'Hold it Pat!'

But Weaver was too drunk with pain and panic to obey any such instruction. He snapped off a shot, hardly even bothering to point the gun before he squeezed the trigger. Glass shattered distantly as the slug pierced a window. Then he lurched heavily to his right, scampering behind a garden shed and scrabbling through the broken fencing into the grounds next door.

Wood shattered as Bodie's shot narrowly missed him, penetrating the shed and finally expending itself on a brick wall.

'Give it up Pat!'

Weaver ran through the gap between the houses, waving his right hand almost uselessly as he snapped off a second shot at Bodie. This one made the CI5 man duck, shoot again towards Weaver, aiming just in front of him. The brickwork exploded in dust and flying shards of clay, which stung Weaver's eyes, making him rub at his face with the back of his hand.

Still he ran.

He came into the road at the front, breath bursting in his lungs, consciousness ebbing from his mind as the blood ebbed from his wounded shoulder.

Ray Doyle stood there, gun aimed, tousled head shaking. 'As far as you go Weaver!'

But Doyle had forgotten another journey that Weaver would shortly be making. For Weaver just fired blindly at Doyle, and though his shot went wild, Doyle was taking no chances.

His return fire lifted Weaver off his feet and flung him two yards backwards, to sprawl at Bodie's feet as Bodie came racing through the side garden. Bodie stared down at the spread-eagled figure, then reached out to close the staring eyes.

He looked up at Ray Doyle, and with no hint of expression on his face said, 'A bit reckless four five.'

'Survival instinct, three seven. I had your position all the time.'

Then they both looked up as the bedroom window was noisily opened. Chrissie Stone looked out at them, and they could see that her face was as white as a sheet. 'I think you'd better come up quick. It's Liz. She's been hit.'

The street around the Stones' house buzzed and crawled with police activity for the next hour. Weaver's body was photographed, and taken away in the second ambulance to arrive on the scene.

The first had screeched away almost within minutes of the shooting, Liz Spalding tucked up safely inside, a half smile on her face. 'I think I'll take up teaching permanently,' she whispered to Bodie, who held her hand as he waited with her on the landing. The wound was not as serious as it had at first seemed, but the bone was broken. It would be a few weeks convalescent leave for the woman, and Bodie already had ideas as to how to help her spend the time.

Dan Monteith appeared on the scene shortly after Weaver's death. He had heard the shooting and come rapidly back towards the house.

In the process he had lost sight of Jack Stone, and Stone had slipped away into the night.

When Cowley arrived on the scene, he shook his head

with irritation, fixing Doyle with a narrow-eyed and angry gaze. 'A fine night's work, Doyle. "Avoid shooting at all costs", and we get an agent out of service, and a dead man. And to cap it all you let a wanted man make good his escape.'

Monteith said, '*I* let him escape, sir. The shooting distracted me.'

'These two were running the show,' said Cowley coldly. 'They take responsibility.'

Doyle, slightly aggrieved, said, 'He can't get far, sir. The police have spread a wide net to snare him.'

'Aye,' said Cowley, pointedly. 'That's what happened the last time, I seem to remember. Jack Stone seems to be the sort of fish that knows how to cut a net or two.'

Exasperated, Doyle said loudly, 'Look, sir. He's berserk about that family of his. The reason he slipped out was to phone and make a few arrangements for them. I guess he didn't trust us to let him do it from the nick. Where's he going to go? He knows his best option, now. I'm sure of it.'

Cowley sighed with irritation, his craggy features registering his unhappiness with his two agents. 'I don't have time to argue with you now. I've just come from the Foreign Office, and you're immediately on a new assignment. You'll be briefed at Control. This is a matter for the police, now.'

'Aye aye, sir,' said Bodie glumly, watching as Cowley moved off towards his limousine. He glanced at Doyle. 'And here I was, thinking that a few hours leave was on the cards.'

'You must be joking,' Doyle said with a sour smile. 'We didn't come up to expectations ... ' his eyes suddenly brightened. 'Though wait a minute. What's this ... ?'

Bodie turned to follow Doyle's gaze. From the darkness between the semi-detached houses across the street came the familiar figure of Jack Stone. He walked solemnly up to Ray Doyle, and smiled thinly.

'I've been watching from across the road. Thought I might have got a chance at Pat Weaver, but you're too efficient for me, Mister Doyle.'

'Nice to see you Jack. Thought you'd flown the coop.'

Stone shook his head. 'Not worth it.' He glanced at the house. 'Can I . . . you know, can I have a few minutes before we go?'

Doyle said, 'Why not? If my colleague here doesn't object.'

Bodie shook his head. 'Help yourself.'

Jack Stone walked quickly to the house, to where Chrissie and the two kids were waiting to say goodbye to him.

# *Chapter Seven*

On the fourth day of the new surveillance, Bodie and Doyle were woken early by Control, and summoned to a briefing session from Cowley's personal assistant. Today was 'pick up' day, no matter what happened. The young revolutionary, whom they had been trailing for sixteen hours a day, was proving less useful than Cowley had hoped, not leading them to any of his more dangerous colleagues.

So the order was changed: follow for an hour, then pick him up. A question and answer session to follow.

By nine that morning they were parked on a side-street off Tottenham Court Road, Bodie at the wheel of the Capri, Doyle slouched down in the passenger seat, idly, almost cursorily, watching the heavy flow of traffic up towards Warren Street. They were waiting for their target to pass, releasing the night-watch man from his stint of duty.

It was a bright day, and Bodie, for all his tiredness, felt quite cheerful. He made idle banter as they watched for the van, and Doyle grimaced and complained about the lack of 'peace and quiet' in that particular car at that particular time.

'You're getting old, Doyle. You're slowing up.'

'No way,' said Doyle. 'Driven to distraction, yes. Slowing up, no.'

'There's our man!'

Doyle had seen it too. A Bedford van, well battered, well seasoned with age and reckless driving. It was coloured a garish blue, an obvious re-spraying job after massive areas of the body-work had been filled in after various collisions. The windows had been tinted purple, and Doyle didn't manage to glimpse the occupants of the cab.

'Here we go again,' said Bodie, as he put the Capri in gear and slid smoothly out into the traffic flow, taking up a surveillance position four cars back from the battered, blue van.

'They'll be going to the Hotel. That means they go through Caplan Street. Quiet, non-residential. We could take them there.' Doyle was thinking out loud. Bodie shook his head.

'The underground car park. Let's go by the book.'

'Enclosed spaces,' said Doyle. 'In our present, trigger-happy moods, it seems a poor selection of place . . . '

'Argument over,' said Bodie, indicating that the van had failed to travel by the obvious route to the Cambridge Hotel.

The van circled the hotel twice, and Bodie dropped back by several cars, suspecting that the van driver was checking for any obvious signs of being followed. Ten minutes later, as he edged and darted through the sluggish traffic that moved along the Marylebone Road, Bodie saw the van turn sharply into the underground car park of the Cambridge, and he went in pursuit.

Doyle checked his forty-five magnum, then slotted it back into the holster on his back belt. Bodie took the Capri down into the basement car park, and squinted through the windscreen, disturbed by the fact that the lights, here, were unusually low. The parking bays were crowded with cars and he drove slowly along the main aisle, while Doyle leaned out of his window, scanning the shadowy depths of the park for a glimpse of their target.

'Hold up,' he said suddenly, and pointed. 'There.'

The van was travelling in parallel to them, but in the opposite direction. It was ascending the half ramp to the next level up.

Doyle saw no sign of any passenger through the darkened side window. 'Move it.'

Without hurrying, without the customary screech of tyres, Bodie guided the Capri round the ramp. The back of the blue van was just vanishing from view.

'That's not the way up,' said Doyle. 'What the hell are they doing?'

Bodie said, 'He's changed his mind. He must have realised he has a tail . . . '

With a screech of brakes, and a squeal of wheels, Bodie reversed into a parking space and shot back along the route he had just taken. The van was clearly headed back towards the exit. Bodie drove recklessly down an 'up' ramp, swerved round one of the thick, concrete pillars and brought the car to a halt, facing the on-coming van.

The van stopped. Doyle watched for movement inside the cab, but saw none. The van's windscreen gleamed darkly in the subdued car-park light. It was a classic face off, and Bodie sensed danger. He opened his door and slipped out of the car, into the protection of the pillar, his gun drawn. Doyle did likewise.

Doyle shouted across the intervening distance. 'You in the van. Out! Now!' As he shouted, Bodie darted a few yards forward, gun held two-handed in front of him, pointed firmly at the windscreen.

He shouted. 'Out you get, boys and girls. Playtime's over.' Doyle moved forward, covered by his partner. They were ten yards from the vehicle. Bodie called, 'Stop playing games. We're not going to hurt you. We just want to talk. Come out *now*! Hands wide and clear.'

'I don't like it,' Doyle murmured, watching the unnervingly silent van.

And suddenly there was action – the van roared into reverse, rushing away from them, its headlights on full beam. It backed into an empty bay, and shot forward and up the ramp again. Bodie loosed off a shot through the back of the vehicle. Doyle's explosive shot starred the side window. Bullet proof glass!

'Get a tyre,' he yelled at Bodie, but Bodie's shot was inches wide, and ricocheted from the concrete wall distantly.

The shattered side window was punched through and a gun barrel appeared. Doyle dived to one side as four quick shots spurted from the ground next to his foot.

Bodie had cut up through the rows of parked cars, swinging up onto the half ramp, and pumping two shots into the van's front tyre. The van slewed wildly, but kept travelling, smoke appearing from its rear tyres as it swerved and skidded back towards the exit.

'We're losing it!' screamed Doyle angrily, darting back towards the Capri. He realised that the van would be clear of the car park before he could get onto the return ramp, and even with its shredded front tyre, it could get outside the hotel area, and the driver escape into the streets of London.

Doyle raced after it. The van had taken the exit into the hotel's rear yard, lurching and swinging towards the open gate that led to Crofton Street. A white-aproned kitchen helper was carrying a huge side of beef from a meat van parked just outside the gate. He had to run for his life as the battered blue vehicle bore down upon him. Doyle appeared in the entrance way to the car park, raised his gun and carefully shot out each of the rear tyres.

The van swerved and crashed into two huge dustbins.

Bodie appeared behind Doyle, grinning. 'Nice shooting.'

'About time. That's shaken them up a bit, I expect.'

They stepped towards the motionless van.

With an ear-shattering explosion, that bowled the CI5 men backwards, the van blew to pieces, black smoke billowing out to fill the kitchen yard!

The Coroner's Court was a drab grey room, cold and bleak, smelling strongly of polish and something more acrid, like disinfectant. Bodie and Ray Doyle sat casually behind the long table that faced the Coroner's desk itself. Cowley sat with them, leaning forward, hands clasped in front of him and resting on his beige folder. He was not a happy man, and the stern set of his jaw, and the way he hardly ever looked at his two operatives, made Ray Doyle realise that the fat was really in the fire this time.

Twice, in less than four days, what should have been a simple operation had turned bad. The driver of the van had been wanted for questioning, and the way CI5 had gone in for the arrest had clearly been the direct cause of the van's destruction on the hot end of the booby-trap bomb it had been carrying.

Ray Doyle was philosophical. There was nothing to be done but face the heat. His boyish features seemed almost bright, almost happy, as he listened to the Coroner questioning a police Inspector, who had been in charge of the Metropolitan Police's part in the operation. The Coroner was in his early forties, a gaunt, greying man, with thick spectacles perched at the very end of his nose. He hardly ever looked up. The same could not be said of his stenographer, seated in front of him.

Bodie was making eyes at the girl, and had been doing so for most of the hearing. She was blonde, pert, and extremely pretty. Doyle dreaded to think of how many mistakes were appearing on the court transcript, each time she looked up at the corner of the room, where the CI5 men sat, and found two youthful, smiling faces, fixing her with meaningful looks.

The only time that Ray Doyle found his composure slipping was when he made the mistake of glancing over his right shoulder, to where the Foreign Office boys were sitting. There were two of them, and themselves they looked young and harmless (which probably meant they weren't either, but Doyle was satisfied to judge by appearances today). It was the oriental gentleman who sat with them that sent the shudders down Doyle's spine.

Colonel Lin Foh. He had been a man in authority in his own country, and used to the arrogant assertion of power . . . and the unquestioning obedience of each and every man who was of lesser rank than him.

He had taken an instant dislike to both Bodie and Doyle, not only because they had bungled the surveillance job on the van containing his potential assassins, but because they dressed casually, more suited to a Sunday afternoon jog than the serious business of the Secret Service.

He had found them scruffy, and had said so in no uncertain terms.

The Coroner was irritated with the proceedings, and with the transparent fact that not all the information that was held by the men in the court-room had been made available to him. He said aloud, 'From all the somewhat diffuse information, indeed, from the *paucity* of information – ' he glanced at Cowley as he said this, 'that has been made available to me, one thing does remain clear. The collision of the van, and the explosion, were intimately connected. The Government Agencies in this case have not been unwilling to provide evidence, I must acknowledge that. But too little seems to have been known to point our thinking in one direction or another: were they killed by their own weapon, or by the weapon of a third party planted within the van?' He checked his notes, and shook his head, glanced at Cowley again, who remained impassively waiting for the proceedings to be officially closed.

'The driver of the vehicle,' the Coroner went on, 'Menni Latowa, had been a student in this country for two and a half years. He was known to be a political activist, but as far as we know had no record of violence. Nor had he any *direct* connection with any terrorist organisation.'

Another pause. Doyle smiled at the stenographer again as she glanced up. There was a satisfying blush on the girl's cheeks.

'Nothing is known about his associate in the vehicle, who remains unidentified. Your investigations, Mister Cowley, have not led us to any further evidence to confirm or clarify the intentions of these men?'

'No, sir. No further evidence.' Cowley spoke softly, firmly, answering with the minimum of words, a pose he had adopted throughout the hearing.

The Coroner looked at the police officers who sat just in front of the Foreign Office representatives. 'And nothing you gentlemen wish to add?' They shook their heads. 'Then I have no alternative, in the circumstances, but to record a verdict of Death by Misadventure. The hearing is closed.'

They all stood, and when the Coroner had left his bench, Ray Doyle walked quickly from the court, Bodie tagging along behind. Cowley had moved off to speak briefly with Colonel Lin Foh.

From the hall outside the court, Doyle peered back into the drab room, wondering whether the girl would reappear, and give him a chance to make his opening.

Bodie said, 'Death by Misadventure.' His voice had a

touch of irony in the tone. 'You play around with bombs, you get blown up.'

Ray Doyle smirked. 'Cynic.'

'Pragmatist,' Bodie corrected.

'I must look that up.' Doyle turned from the door and walked towards the exit. He would call back another day, he'd decided. He had some chores to do now, before facing Cowley back at the office.

Bodie grinned. 'As soon as you've gone, she'll be out of here like a flash. You must learn to recognise when a woman's look is one of despair, not lust.'

'Oh yeah! Body language ... '

They walked outside, into the bright, clear day. 'How about a drink? Can't make language any clearer than that!'

Doyle shook his head. 'No. Things to do first. My bachelor's life is catching up on me.'

'One on the corner. To discuss our plan of action with Cowley.'

'Too many things to do,' said Doyle, zipping up his black leather windcheater. 'I didn't expect this extra bit of spare time.'

'Can we help it if the job blew up in our faces?'

With a grin, Doyle added, 'It's an ill wind. See you.'

'Yeah. Have fun at the supermarket.'

Bodie walked off to his car, parked at the edge of the cemetery that backed the Coroner's Court building. Doyle was parked further away, and he cut round the side road, walking briskly alongside the high, wooden fence.

As he reached his car he stopped, his hand on the key in the lock. Looking back along the road he frowned. He had felt uncomfortable for a moment, the nasty sensation of being watched. There was no one around. Distantly, he saw Bodie's Capri roaring off up the street. There were several cars, and one small van, parked nearby, but they were all empty.

Quickly, Doyle unlocked his car and climbed in. 'You need a holiday, son,' he said to himself as he pulled away from the kerb. 'You're getting jumpy.'

Colonel Lin Foh, formerly of the Military Intelligence Agency of his remote sub-tropical country, a man of wealth, breeding, and once among the most important functionaries of his State, was furious. And his anger was totally directed at George Cowley.

As head of CI5, Cowley had assumed the responsibility for the protection of the Colonel, a guest in the country. It was one of CI5's many 'dirty tasks' to afford protection for the lives of exiles, visitors from repressive Governments, and the representatives of Governments with which Britain maintained the most reluctant and tenuous of diplomatic relations.

Such men were dangerous, and were in danger. CI5 took the responsibility for ensuring that no harm came to, or from, those ill-favoured dignitaries.

Colonel Lin Foh had no idea of the contempt with which he, and his fallen Government, had been held by the British Government itself. All he knew was that he had been inadequately protected, and that an attempt on his life had been thwarted by the merest accident.

He did not like the fact that his potential assassins had got so close to the Hotel where he was staying.

He shouted at Cowley in a high-pitched, almost hysterical fashion, his oriental face flushed bright red, his fists clenched by his sides.

Cowley waited for the fury to abate, staring impassively at the little man. When Lin Foh had paused for breath, Cowley smiled.

'You have perfectly adequate protection, Colonel,' he said in his infuriatingly soft tone of voice, the abrasive Scots edge he could so easily manage gone to be replaced by a soothing, British unflappability. 'You have round-the-clock protection.'

'One man!' screeched Lin Foh, and slapped his sides in exasperation. 'A bodyguard of one man! In my country a man of my rank would be screened completely from any *possible* risk of attack!'

Coolly, Cowley replied, 'You are not in your own country now, Colonel Lin Foh. The exceptional talents of CI5 are spread quite thin in the pursuit of protection for all manner of important persons, from very many different nations.'

'But I am your guest! I am in your country! You invited me here, and you should afford me the protection due a man of my rank, and status.'

With a quick, firm shake of his head, Cowley said, 'No sir. You were not invited to our country. You were permitted to enter.' Lin Foh looked shocked as Cowley stated the unstatable, heavily implying that Lin Foh was not a welcome presence in England, after the coup that had ousted the ruling junta two months before. 'You were permitted to enter the country,' Cowley repeated, 'as a visitor. To receive medical treatment, which is now completed. Satisfactorily completed, I hope.'

Lin Foh jerked his head in acknowledgement of the courtesy, his princely bearing enabling him to do nothing else. 'Yes. Thank you. But Mister Cowley, I must repeat. That bomb was certainly meant for me. You know it full well. There was no one else in the hotel who could have been of any possible interest to the assassins.'

Cowley acknowledged that. 'Always assuming, Colonel, that their prospective target was *in* the hotel. It could equally be that they had spotted my men following them and were attempting to shake them off.'

Lin Foh hesitated, frowned, then glanced back at the two young Foreign Office men; they were hardly protection for the Colonel; rather, were deliberately overt presences with him, keeping an eye on him on the instruction of the Foreign Secretary. Lin Foh did not trust them, and walked forward, encouraging Cowley to walk with him, ahead of the other two.

'Why were your men following the assassins?'

Cowley said, 'Simply for information, Colonel. We knew that there was a current of dissenion about your arrival in England, and our Intelligence made it clear that there would be demonstrations against you.'

Lin Foh seemed incensed, but kept his voice down as they reached the outside steps of the Coroner's Court. His CI5 bodyguard was waiting there, a cool-looking Welshman called Evans, his nose buried in a cheap hack novel which he hastily pushed into his inside pocket as Lin Foh and Cowley appeared.

'What I don't understand, Major Cowley, is that if you *know* my life is in danger, why do I have just *one man*!?' He glanced at Cowley, sensing the disapproval in the calm man's face. 'I think I understand. For years the Government I served was a popular one with the people – but not with the British Government. Now *rabble* run my country. But that rabble are seen by you *heart-aching* British as more truly democratic than the authoritarian rule of the Military, even though we respected the people's rights in accordance with every convention. The quality of your protection is subject to your moralising attitude on the way a country is run!'

'I'm not a politician, Colonel,' said Cowley coldly.

'We have all been branded murderers,' Lin Foh persisted. 'Your Government listens to the terrorist propaganda. We are in exile, or we are dead, those of us who ruled firmly but fairly. I am from a line of Princes, Major Cowley. I am not afraid to die. But not wastefully. If I were still a Minister of my country you would be giving me real protection, day and night. I want that now.'

Tired of the wheedling tone, the persistent arrogance of the man, Cowley lost his cool and turned on the colonel. 'You listen to me, Colonel Lin Foh. My Government accepted your presence here despite warnings as to what might happen if they did so!' Lin Foh blinked, quite astonished at being spoken to so sharply. Cowley went on. 'Because, Colonel, we will not be dictated to, certainly not by blackmailers with bombs in their hands – '

'Major Cowley!'

'Colonel Lin Foh! Let me finish! We will not let *you* invade our streets either. We've had enough. If you want to kill each other, then go home and do it. Not here. I don't know why they want to kill you, Colonel. I don't know why you would want to kill them, but I'm sure that you would if you had them in your hands. The bodies of two young boys have been stitched back together in the mortuary of this place. Did you see them, Colonel? A most disgusting sight. We don't want any more bodies. Not yours, not mine, not some poor kid, or beggar, or tramp, or old lady that happens to get in the line of fire.'

Lin Foh said nothing, stood stiffly to attention and stared at Cowley as Cowley said his piece.

George Cowley summed up. 'We don't want your war here, Colonel. I am authorised to tell you that my Government is very happy that your treatment has been successful and we hope that as soon as your medical advisers deem you fit to travel, you will make arrangements and leave.'

Colonel Lin Foh's eyes widened, his lips parted in unspoken protest, but only the feeble question, 'Leave to go where?' emerged.

'Your Government had many friends in South East Asia. I am sure one of them would afford you the protection that you seek. Until then, one of my men will stay with you as before. Not for your sake, Colonel, but because we prefer to keep peace on the streets.'

Try as he would, Ray Doyle could not shake the sensation of being watched.

He drove slowly towards his area of London, running through in his mind all the things he needed to buy and do during this free afternoon.

But all the time he found his eyes fixed to the rear mirror, looking for a sign of pursuit. He tried everything, turning corners and stopping abruptly, but there was no tangible sign of a pursuer anywhere.

When he parked outside a row of shops, he stood for a moment examining the passing traffic. Except for a white, Ford van, similar to the van that had been parked near to the Coroner's Court, nothing caught his suspicions; he watched the van drive past. It continued on down the street and vanished into the distance. The shadowy features of the driver had clearly been fixed upon the road ahead.

Nerves, he thought to himself. It's lack of sleep, two

surveillance missions gone a little wrong – well, all right, a lot wrong. It's tiredness and tension.

There's no one watching me at all.

He bought groceries to last him the week, then popped next door to the frame shop to pick up the stainless steel frame he'd ordered for a James Barker black and white print he'd obtained in an auction some weeks before. Doyle was beginning to fancy himself as a small-time connoisseur of Modern Alternative Art.

From the shops it was a short visit to the launderette, where his week's supply of dirty washing had been cleaned, pressed and packed for him by the friendly woman who supervised the place. He chatted with her for a few minutes, then placed the bag of clothes into the boot of his car, and headed for home.

The sensation of being observed had gone at last. He chuckled to himself as he drove, and had forgotten his worries by the time he had hauled two armfuls of grocery supplies up to his apartment.

He struggled to unlock the door, manipulating the key in the yale lock with difficulty. He realised, with a thrill of annoyance at himself, that in his haste – his weary haste – to get to the hearing that morning, he had omitted to set the second lock with its automatic alarm connection.

'You're slipping, Doyle. You *do* need a holiday.'

As the door swung open he pushed it with his back and entered the darkened apartment. The curtains were still pulled and he placed one of the packages of groceries on the table, holding the other to his side as he went across the room and whipped back the heavy green curtains.

Light spilled into the flat, illuminating the untidy lounge. Doyle shook his head as he contemplated the mess, then he walked back to the table to take the supplies into the kitchen . . .

Movement from the bedroom . . .

He stopped, glanced towards the half-open door, and all the blood drained from his face as he realised that someone was standing there, out of sight.

'Who the hell . . . ?' he began, and his eyes widened with shock.

The silenced muzzle of a gun stabbed out of the darkness and spat twice. Doyle was flung back across the table, a milk bottle exploding in the bag he held across his chest. Glass and white liquid splashed outwards. The groceries scattered. Blood mixed with the milk.

The first two shots took him in the shoulder and the left chest. The third shot struck a large bottle-garden on the side-board, and the glass shattered spectacularly, showering green shards and dark, moist earth onto the tumbling form of the man. The fourth shot struck again in the chest, slamming Doyle hard against the wall, leaving a bloody smear as he slowly slipped to the floor, his eyes half closed, the breath wheezing from his lungs.

The figure of his assassin grew large above him, a dark shape, peering down, the gun raised for the *coup-de-grace*. Doyle turned his head and closed his eyes, and the quiet discharge from the silenced thirty-eight was the last sound he heard . . .

Except for the ansaphone buzzing, and the vibration on the floor of his assailant moving rapidly towards the french windows, to make good an escape down the back way.

## *Chapter Eight*

A small room below the Operations Centre at CI5: a room laid out like a telephone exchange, with junction boxes on the wall, and switchboards built into the smooth panels that were the work surfaces; a quiet room, save for the hiss of the air conditioning and the easy movements of two men in chairs, monitoring flickering TV screens.

At one side of the room, on a panel of lights, a light glowed red, then began to flicker on and off. At the same time a gentle bell sounded, causing both men to look round in surprise.

One of them reacted at once, rising quickly from his station, crossing the room and checking the number below the flashing light. He ran his finger down a list of names on a clip-board.

'Ray Doyle . . . ' he murmured. 'Priority Red. Punch that through, will you?'

The other man nodded silently and tapped out the signal on a key-board built into his desk. The first watcher picked up the red phone nearby and punched out three digits. He raised the receiver to his ear and waited, his face pale in the subdued light of the room, impatience beginning to mark lines at the edge of his lips.

The car phone in Cowley's small, private vehicle blinked red. Cowley stood some way away, outside offices in Whitehall. He was talking with a tall, overweight man, dressed in Whitehall pin-stripe and bowler hat. The conversation was animated, almost angry, and Cowley stared at his opponent with his rugged features etched strongly with irritation.

The blinking red light was not out of view; but Cowley never looked towards his car, never noticed the light, like a heartbeat, urgently pumping, urgently calling ...

Three more digits. An exhalation of irritation, a sense of panic in the man who was trained to recognise, to intuit, the signs of danger, the signals of need ...

Bodie stepped from his car, waiting for a bus to pass, then darted across the street to the antique shop called Old Peculiar.

Behind him, the red light on his car phone began to blink. Bodie pushed into the shop. In the reflection on the glass door he thought he saw a red glow from his car, and glanced back across the road. A bus was passing between him and the parked vehicle, and he hesitated ...

A voice said, 'Oh, hello Bodie. Nice to see you.'

He smiled and turned back into the shop, to greet the woman who stood there.

Red light flashing. Silently blinking. Reflected in the half opened eyes of the man who lay dying on the thick rug of his apartment.

He had no voice. The telephone receiver dangled uselessly some feet from his motionless body. It had been knocked from its cradle when he had gone over with the first shot. His lips moved, framing words, but there was no strength in him to make the air push forward and give sound to the desperate message he was trying to call ...

The red light winked. Control were trying to get hold of him, to verify that he had accidentally triggered his window alarm. When no verification came, they would send someone round.

Wouldn't they?

*Bodie! Bodie, where the hell are you?*

Red light blinking. On, off. One, two. One, two. Heartbeat slowing, the blood oozing from three holes in his body, spreading out to mingle with the drying milk, the gleaming shards of glass.

*He rose from the muddy ground and began to run towards the woodland. There was movement there, and he raised his machine pistol and pumped a burst of fire into the bush where the man was crouching. There was a scream of pain. Movement to the right. The mud churned and erupted as bullets struck the ground, and he rolled to his left, lay sprawled on his stomach, and pumped fire into the running shape of the man who had nearly killed him . . .*

Images:

A hand raised in the darkened doorway of a room; light gleamed on the smooth metal barrel of a gun. Bright flashes of light, the silent spit of .38 calibre rounds . . .

Explosion of glass. The thump of a fist on his shoulder. The thump of the wall against his back. Furtive movement. The gaping round mouth of the gun, centred squarely on his left eye. Finger tightening on trigger.

*Final shot!*

No! Not yet! Not ready! To die! Not yet!

*Bodie! I need you, dammit. Bodie!*

One, two, the bullet went through . . .

Three, four, there's blood on the floor, on the floor . . .

George Cowley was furious. He left the Home Office official, very dissatisfied with the man's unhelpful attitude towards Colonel Lin Foh. In Cowley's opinion, the arrogant little man should be invited to leave the country in the very near future indeed. The Home Office were not prepared to enforce such a departure, however, until the appropriate word had been received from their colleagues in the Foreign affairs department.

Cowley left the man, and returned to his car. He noticed that the phone was ringing, and as he sat down he picked up the receiver and almost casually identified himself.

A moment later he was red-faced, reacting with a panic that was quite exceptional for George Cowley.

'Why the Devil wasn't I informed at once?'

'You had already left the Minister's office, sir . . . '

He pushed the car into gear, and swung out into the traffic near Westminster. 'Are you sure it's Doyle's voice?'

'Pretty sure,' came the voice of the man at Control. 'It's very faint, very weak. It took a while to get the line opened.

He must have knocked the receiver from its cradle. He sounds bad . . . '

'Right. Raise Bodie!'

'We've just located him, sir. He's on his way. There's an ambulance on its way too, and we've informed the Met. They're standing by.'

'Good. Out.'

Bodie raced up the stairs to Doyle's apartment, and rang the buzzer furiously, stabbing the button as if he could make the door open by doing so.

There was no response.

He fumbled for his skeleton keys and realised that he had not brought them with him from the car. His R/T was still below as well.

Nothing for it. It would have to be the balcony, and the french windows.

He pulled open the landing window and edged out onto the ledge which ran around the block. He climbed onto the balcony of the neighbouring flat to Doyle's, then edged along to the small terrace where Doyle kept his garden.

Opposite him a woman leaned out of the window of her own apartment and shouted at him. 'You! You there! Get away from there!'

Shut up you old bag, Bodie thought viciously, and ignored her. Her voice carried on the still air. 'Call for the Police. It's a burglar! Get the Police, somebody.'

Bodie jumped quickly onto Doyle's terrace. The french windows were closed and he drew his gun and peered in to the gloomy apartment.

All was silent and still inside.

Then he saw the hand, its fingers curled, as if trying to drag the sprawled body that was attached to it across the room. 'Oh Christ!'

Still cautious, but now feeling the blood drain from his face with shock, Bodie moved quickly into the flat. He kicked open the doors to bedroom and kitchen, established that there was no one hiding behind them, and then raced across to kneel by Ray Doyle.

He picked up Doyle's limp hand and felt for a pulse. It was feeble, but quite regular. He touched Doyle's shoulder and saw the two gaping wounds, then noticed the third in the chest, above the heart.

'You're a damn lucky man, Doyle. An inch lower and that would have been fatal.'

He stared at his unconscious friend. Doyle's eyes were half open, but there was no awareness, no recognition in them.

*Where was that damn ambulance?*

He fetched a blanket from the bedroom and wrapped it round Doyle's body, trying not to touch the wounds. Then he placed the phone back on the hook, waited a second, and dialled. 'Priority A-3,' he reported to Control. 'We need emergency hospital action. Fix it up?'

'Consider it done,' said Control. 'How's he look?'

'He's taken three, one near the heart. He's going fast.' As he placed the phone back down, Bodie heard a strange sound, like hailstones striking glass.

He glanced at Ray Doyle, and realised that Doyle was conscious and shivering, his teeth chattering violently as he stared up at his colleague.

Bodie dropped to a crouch and took Doyle's hand in his, pressing the cold flesh to try and keep the circulation going. Doyle watched him and the shivering died down.

Bodie said, 'Can't leave you alone for a minute.'

The hand that he held clenched slightly, a weak movement, but a clear and welcome acknowledgement of Bodie's presence.

Bodie waited by his friend. He wondered what was going through Doyle's mind, what scenes of terror and survival, what images reflecting the desperate fight for life . . .

*Doyle stepped into the club bar, looked around and finally saw his new partner sitting at the bar itself, slowly drinking a pint of orange juice.*

*So that's Bodie. Ugly looking customer.*

*Bodie was in squash gear, still holding his racquet across his knees. Sweat had stained his shirt and as Doyle approached he could smell the effort on the man's body. He wrinkled his nose as he came up to the other man.*

*'Is it always going to be like this? Or will you have the occasional bath?'*

*Bodie kept drinking as he eyed the newcomer. Smacking his lips he placed the empty glass down on the bar. 'Sweat it out, pour it back. Gotta keep cool.'*

*They eyed each other, assessing the signs of strength in the face, the hands, the bearing; looking for the weaknesses that they would have to live with, now that they were a team.*

*'Ray Doyle,' said Doyle, and extended his hand.*

*'Who else?' said Bodie, and added with a smile, 'Call me Bodie. I like it better than the other tag.'*

*Doyle looked down at his hand, smeared with sweat. 'How long did you play?'*

*'An hour. Fitness is the most important thing I know. Can never dare lose it. You fit?'*

*Doyle shrugged. He liked the smooth-featured, sharp-eyed man, despite the reek of sweat and exertion. Bodie seemed to be warming to him, too.*

*He shrugged. 'Couldn't play squash for an hour. Mug's game, over-doing it.'*

*'I quite agree. But I'm different to you. I'm cool. Bodywise, that is. I sneaked a look at my medical report: slow heartbeat, low metabolism. I was born cool . . . '*

*Doyle smiled thinly. 'I suppose you sneaked a look at mine too.'*

*Bodie affirmed that with an inclination of his head. 'Very* uncool. *But you're one of the best. Top of the pile. You don't fall when they push. That's important. And you don't give a damn. That's important too. Can't afford to give a damn. Not too much, anyway. Might make you hesitate. Never mind the book, aim at the heart, shoot to kill, the other guy will . . . '*

*Doyle said. 'Very useful advice. Shame I already got it from Cowley. Anyway, when're you going to stop talking and get me a drink? A man could die of heat-stroke, standing around you . . .'*

The fantasy faded from Doyle's shadowed, fevered mind. A

moment of clarity touched him, and his eyes flickered open, and managed to focus on the roof of the vehicle that sped him westwards, towards the hospital.

*An ambulance*, he thought. *I'm on my way.*

He could hear the siren, was vaguely conscious of a flickering blue light. Above him hung a cellophane bag of yellowy liquid, a tube carrying that vital plasma into his arm, somewhere below the lower extent of his field of vision. The ambulance veered and swerved and he felt his body move slightly on the hard bunk.

He was warm. He felt alive, but very weak. The images from his eyes faded and blurred. Somewhere, distantly, he could hear the rush of sea, and the steady thump of the living earth, a strange, regular drum beat, that seemed to expand to fill his mind.

And Bodie was there, leaning close, face solemn, but concern and anguish clearly evident in his dark eyes.

'Doyle! Ray! Can you hear me?'

*Course I can hear you. Idiot!*

But the affectionate insult remained trapped in Doyle's mind. His lips wouldn't move to give voice to the words.

'Who was it?' Bodie urged. 'Did you see who shot you? Come on, for Chrissake! Who did this to you, Ray?'

A hand on his own. Doyle twitched and flexed his fingers, trying to communicate to Bodie in the only way possible. Bodie watched the hand, then quietly sighed, sat back against the side of the ambulance and stared at his friend.

George Cowley arrived at the hospital just as Doyle's now unconscious body was being wheeled into the emergency operating room. Two brisk, efficient looking nurses had taken Doyle's vital signs, changed the plasma drip, and generally prepared the man for surgery. As Cowley walked towards the slightly hunched figure of Bodie, he was able to see Doyle's peaceful face, eyes closed, white as a sheet; a moment later the trolley was behind the closing doors of the lift, and Doyle's life was now in the hands of others, men skilled in surgery, and in the ways of keeping the tenuous thread of life attached to a dying body.

'What about his chances?' Cowley asked gruffly, as Bodie turned to acknowledge him. Bodie shook his head.

'Not good. But not hopeless. But what can they say? They're keeping hope alive, that's all.'

'How many did he take?'

'Three. One's in his chest, still lodged. One in his shoulder. One passed through.'

They walked back to the waiting area. Bodie felt his hands shaking, with nerves, and with anger.

Cowley suddenly said, 'You're off all other assignments, Bodie. I want whoever it was did this to Doyle. Any ideas?'

'Clumsy job. Not an expert who shot him. A professional would have delivered the final shot to the head.'

'I agree,' said Cowley stiffly.

Bodie shrugged. 'I wouldn't say it was a regular break-in, thief surprised and shoots out of panic. Maybe someone with an old score to settle?'

'Or something more random. Did you come straight here?'

Bodie nodded. 'With the ambulance.'

'So you haven't searched the flat?'

Searching the flat had been the last thing on his mind, but Bodie said, 'Malone's boys are on it now.'

Cowley made a sound of irritated dismissal. 'Malone! I want *you* to search it, Bodie. You! You know the man.'

Uncomfortable, not liking the thought of leaving the hospital until he knew the worst . . . or best . . . Bodie said, 'I think I'd like to hang on here for a bit.'

'And do what?' Cowley shook his head, sympathetic though he was to Bodie's feelings. 'There's nothing you can do here. Come on. I'll come with you to the flat.'

The police had already been very thorough by the time Bodie and Cowley gained access to Doyle's cordoned off apartment. A police photographer was just finishing up in the corner of the room where Doyle had fallen. Two uniformed men were on their hands and knees, brushing at the carpet with their fingers. A plainclothes man was examining the french windows.

Inspector Malone came across to Cowley immediately. 'Afternoon, sir.'

'How'd they get in?' asked Cowley, getting straight to the point.

'Ordinary combination key, we think. No sign of breaking and entering.'

'That means Doyle didn't set the second locks.'

Bodie said, 'He wasn't expecting anything. He's done it before. Laziness ... '

Malone said, 'Made it easy for them to get in.'

Frowning, Cowley asked, 'Why "they"? You think there were more than one?'

'Hard to tell. No sign of fingerprints. Only one gun used. But the alarm wasn't triggered until they went out through the window.'

'Neighbours hear anything?'

Malone shook his head. 'Silencer, obviously. But there's these ... ' He produced a cellophane bag containing two spent bullets. 'Dug these out of the wall. One of them went through the body first.'

Taking the bag and holding it up towards the window, Bodie peered at the two slugs. 'Thirty-eight calibre. What the hell are they doing in your pocket? Why aren't they at ballistics?'

'All right, all right!' said Malone irritatedly. 'We've only just dug them out, Bodie.'

'Yeah. Sorry.'

'This is just a preliminary going over. There's a lot more to do, yet.'

Cowley walked into the bedroom, Bodie following. Bodie said, 'Nothing's been touched. If they were looking for something they knew where it was. But what could he have had that they wanted?'

Cowley was standing staring at a painted Asian doll on the sideboard. 'Just his life, perhaps.'

Looking grim as he glanced out of the small, bedroom window, Bodie nodded. 'Well they haven't got it yet!' Memories of shared evenings, with cans of beer and football on the TV, flooded back to Bodie; shared hours with Ray

Doyle, mad pursuits, of cars, of women, shared jokes, anger, support; he knew this small apartment almost as well as he knew his own. It didn't seem right that Ray Doyle might never again come staggering out of the untidy bedroom, curly hair looking a totally dishevelled mess, eyes bleary, to find Bodie sprawled on the settee, bright and cheery and grinning. He struck the window frame with his fist.

Cowley looked round sharply. 'No vendettas, Bodie. No revenge. Whatever happens to Doyle, it was his job. Remember that. It was his job, and risks and death come with that job.'

'What, being the target for a political loony? That's part of the job?'

'You're making presumptions, Bodie. Political loony, surprised thief, old lag with a grudge . . . it's facts I want, not surmise. Stay on it. I'm going back to the hospital.'

And he left Bodie standing in the shadows of the room, still staring out of the window.

From the small gallery above the operating theatre the whole process was obscure, if sickeningly bloody, to the watching Cowley. He sat where medical students usually sat, hands clasped before him, watching the rapid movement of the green-robed figures below. He could see Doyle's curly hair, but the man's face was hidden by the anaesthetist's mask. Screens flickered with light. Nurses moved efficiently about. Two white-haired surgeons were bent over Doyle's open chest, probing in the cavity around the heart.

Their words, the sound of the life-support machine, the murmurs of weariness and exasperation from the operating team, all of these things came to Cowley through the amplifiers in the gallery. He had asked for it to be so.

Eventually he heard the cultured tones of the Consultant Surgeon, Edward Siegel. 'There it is. Just behind the valve. It's lodged . . . '

There was a sudden slowing in the regular tone that signalled Doyle's heart-beat. The anaesthetist said urgently 'I'm losing him.'

Siegel snapped back, 'No you're not. I need a minute, fifty seconds. Keep him alive for fifty seconds. Nurse! Stimulate! Quickly!'

A nurse moved to the life support machine and flipped a switch. Doyle's body jerked on the operating table.

Siegel said loudly, 'The man's not trying! Again. Stimulate again!'

Bodie entered the gallery and sat down next to Cowley, grimacing as he saw the open-heart operation below. Cowley looked up, looked grim. 'It's touch and go, Bodie.'

'He'll make it.'

Sighing, Cowley looked back down at the operation. 'Will he? Does he want to? How strong's his will?'

'The strongest.'

'I'm not so sure. He's not cold-blooded enough. There's not enough of the animal in him. Too much imagination. It might seem too easy to him just to slip away into the fantasy world of death.' He looked round at Bodie. 'Never mind me. I'm in a precious maudlin mood. What have you got?'

'Ballistics ran a make on those bullets. Match with one picked up in Amsterdam six weeks ago.'

'Picked up? Or picked out . . . of who?'

'The Italian Chargé d'Affaires.'

'Aha.' Cowley nodded thoughtfully. Bodie prompted, 'How does that connect up with Doyle?'

'The bullet in the wall, Bodie. The second bullet. I spoke with the forensic boys. The second bullet was fired from close to where Doyle was lying, and at a very steep angle. Doyle was alive, manifestly alive. And the final shot missed totally, from just above his body. If you saw your target still breathing, what would you do?'

'One to the head, to finish him off.'

'Precisely. Our man, whoever he is, came in close for the kill, but couldn't go through with it.'

Bodie nodded as he thought through the implications of that. 'No stomach for a cold-blooded assassination. Hesitant. Three shots to the body, hoping for a kill from a distance. But failed. And then the reality was too strong to stomach.'

Cowley watched as the surgeon, below, dropped the bloodied bullet from Doyle's heart into a silver dish.

'I think we have a chance at last, Bodie. A real chance.'

## *Chapter Nine*

The hospital room, in intensive care, where Ray Doyle lay in a state somewhere equally between life and death, was decked out like the inside of a spaceship. Wires, screens, machines and consoles surrounded the bed where the supine body lay.

Doyle's breathing was easy, his heart-beat slow, irregular. A nurse sat beside him, her attention fixed firmly on the signals and lines on the screen, the visible evidence of Doyle's fight for life.

Edward Siegel, tired after the operation, explained to Cowley that, 'His system is basically dormant. Idling. It's just doing enough to keep him alive. But the brain activity ... ' He pointed to one of the monitor screens. 'The brain is the first organ to truly "die". It's a romantic notion I know – but to me, with his system idling yet the brain activity so intense, I think it's as if he's trying to come to a decision.'

Understanding what the doctor was saying, Cowley nodded grimly. 'Whether to live or die, you mean?'

'Precisely. He's arguing with himself. He needs auditory input from people who care, who love him. Wife?'

'No wife. And I don't think he's had a deep relationship for some time. I'll chase his parents.' Cowley walked to the bed and stared at the silent man. 'He's done more, seen more, to make him want to toss it all in than almost anybody his age. He's an idealist. Aspects of his work, his life style, are disagreeable to him in the extreme. He may be judging whether or not it's worth returning to it.'

Siegel said softly, 'If that's the case, let's hope there is something in his life that he would miss too much to let it go so easily ... '

While Ray Doyle struggled for his life in the Intensive Care

Unit, in the computer room at CI5 headquarters, George Cowley and Bodie struggled to find the 'connection'. Bodie was reading through a stack of reports on International Terrorist presences in the United Kingdom. Cowley was talking with Interpol on the phone.

When the call was finished he walked over in his shirt-sleeves to where Bodie was stretched out in an office chair, feet on a desk. Cowley said, 'It's the same thing all over: Paris, Amsterdam, Rome, Berlin ... a lot of refugee students, mostly kicked out by Lin Foh's military Government. They're not short of cash. So far their reaction to the take-over has been loudly-voiced support, and angrily expressed sentiments of violence, but no violence itself. The so-called gangsters, like Colonel Lin Foh, are all being threatened with reprisals ... '

'But nobody's losing much sleep over it,' added Bodie, 'except us.'

'Indeed,' said Cowley, seating himself on the edge of the desk. 'So what have we got?'

Putting his hands behind his head, Bodie stretched back and narrowed his eyes. 'Two bullets from a gun fired in Amsterdam; Ray Doyle dying; and we *would* have had Menni Latowa, which would have stopped all this, *if* we hadn't decided to bring him in too late.'

Sensing a certain self-irritation in Bodie's tone of voice, Cowley said quickly, firmly, 'They were my orders, Bodie. We had Latowa listed as one of the "Big Talk, Big Ideal, Big Dreams" type. Harmless in himself – we thought – he would lead us to the dangerous ones if there were any. That's why you were tailing him. That was *my* mistake, if mistake it was, not yours.'

Fiercely, Bodie said, 'I wasn't blaming myself.' He swung his legs from the desk, and stared at Cowley through dark, angry eyes.

Cowley responded almost with a shout, 'I know damn well what you were doing! And you should have put it in writing if you'd wanted to make anything of it!'

Bodie calmed down, and Cowley followed suit. There was

a strained pause as temperatures lowered, then Cowley said, 'Okay. Let's run through it again. Latowa and the unknown "Charlie" who died with him, were carrying a bomb designed for Colonel Lin Foh.'

'You think so?'

'No question about it. I don't believe in coincidences, Bodie. Connection. You and Doyle were following Latowa, the only student we knew of with any sort of *modus operandi*. Connection?'

'Charlie. His mate.'

Cowley tapped a finger on his knee. 'Charlie. Unidentified Caucasian, aged about 28. Logically Charlie would have to be the bomb maker.'

'Because in the four days Doyle and me were following Latowa, he and Charlie only met twice - once for about thirty seconds, probably just to say hello, and then to go to the Cambridge Hotel.'

Cowley nodded. 'Connection?'

Bodie said, 'Bullets from the same gun that killed the Italian Chargé d'Affaires, dug out of Doyle's heart.'

'The same gun,' Cowley emphasised. 'Not necessarily the same person ... unless it were a friend of Charlie's. Connection? Some of the students were getting ready to do more than talk. They'd joined the International Terrorist Freemasonry ... '

'And they supplied Latowa with expertise and supplies: Charlie himself, the bomb maker; guns; ammunition ... but in exchange for what?'

Cowley said, 'The continuing revolution. Civil unrest. The breakdown of social stability. Anywhere. Isn't that what they're all after?' Cowley was liking the sound of this; ideas and facts were beginning to fit together. 'So we have a connection closer to home: Doyle saw something that threatened them. Or someone. Not Latowa, he's dead. So is Charlie. Someone, then, who you met during the surveillance of Latowa. Someone who would recognise Doyle. Someone, perhaps, who was tailing *you* while you tailed Latowa, and saw the explosion, and is out for revenge. You were always with Doyle? You saw all the same people?'

'Yeah. So why is Doyle hit and not me?'

With a shrug, and a solemn-faced little glance at Bodie, Cowley said, 'Unless you're next on the list.'

Bodie shivered at the thought of undergoing the same operation as his colleague. Then a thought struck him. 'There *was* someone I didn't actually *see*. Doyle saw her . . .'

'Go on,' said Cowley, interested suddenly.

'It's in our report,' Bodie said.

'My mind's not a computer, Bodie. I don't remember every single item in every untidy report that the two of you have ever put in. Tell me about it . . . '

Bodie leaned back, got his thoughts in order. 'We were tailing the van. This is three days before the explosion. We were following into Camden Lock . . . '

Bodie stopped the car at a discreet distance from Latowa's blue van, and watched as Latowa got out of the cab and walked into one of the shops in the small row. They were close to the canal, and there were several people about, inspecting the expensive fashion jewellery on sale in several shops, or just enjoying the peaceful atmosphere of the lock area.

Latowa came out of the shop with a dusky skinned Asiatic man, and the conversation was animated, if inaudible. It was clear to Doyle that Latowa's contact was not at all happy to see him.

Bodie got out of the car and strolled past the two men, standing quite close to them and browsing in the window of the shop before which they stood. The shop was an AgitProp bookshop, a place to buy the works of the various revolutionaries, as well as pamphlets from the hundreds of radical International political movements around the world.

Doyle left the car too and stepped into an oriental bric-à-brac shop. From here he could see the two talking men quite clearly, and he picked up various objects on display, looking at them quite interestedly, and keeping only half an eye on the scene outside.

This was the sort of shop he liked, with its range of hand made jewellery in the oriental tradition, prints and puppets, and odd items of no functional use whatsoever, but attractive in that they reflected a long vanished Eastern culture.

He had just picked up a particularly attractive ring, when a girl's voice said, 'That's not for sale.'

Doyle looked round and saw her. She was almost hidden behind a display of dolls and puppets, and was painting the facial features on an exotic looking doll.

'I rather liked it,' he said. She was very pretty, this girl, dressed in a bright green cheong sam, her dark hair gleaming with natural oil, and framing a pert, oriental face.

'It's mine. I took it off to paint the doll. Sorry.' She smiled sweetly. Doyle shrugged, looked at the ring.

'Very precious?'

'No. Very ordinary. But please choose another ring. They are all very pretty.'

'But this is the one I want. Really.' He tossed the girl's ring into the air and caught it, grinning at her.

Bodie had walked back to the car, and sat quietly watching the propagandist book shop, and the still-talking forms of Latowa and the young man, now inside the premises. Doyle climbed into the car carrying the doll that the girl had been painting, and the ring that they had argued about. 'Who is he?' Doyle asked, nodding towards the man with Latowa.

'Edits some South East Asian news-sheet.'

'Friendly quarrel?'

Bodie shrugged and glanced at the doll. 'What the hell's that?'

Doyle showed the ring. 'I wanted this.' He held up the doll. 'I had to buy this to get it. It's called bartering.'

'Gullibility more like.'

Two more days of routine surveillance followed. Then, the day before Latowa's death, he made his first contact with 'Charlie'.

Doyle was at the wheel, following through the Earl's Court area. The blue van, driven by Latowa, pulled up outside a tall, ramshackle house, long ago turned into bedsitters. Doyle swung the car into the kerb, and observed cautiously through the windscreens of the intervening parked vehicles.

'Charlie' appeared almost immediately, a tall, lanky youth, looking younger on the surface than the autopsy would later place him. He was dressed in a black leather windcheater, black cords, and carried an airline bag.

He got into the van for less than a minute, then went back to his room, and Latowa drove off. He was not carrying the airline bag when he took his leave of Latowa.

And it was as Doyle swung the car out into the traffic again that he glimpsed the girl from the oriental-art shop. Or at least, glimpsed someone who looked remarkably like her.

'What's up?' Bodie asked, as Doyle hesitated, half out into the road, looking back over his shoulder.

'The girl from the shop ... I thought I saw her ... '

Bodie looked and saw the back of a dark-haired girl, just disappearing into a small, white van. 'Hey,' he said, tapping Doyle on the shoulder. 'We have a pursuit, remember?'

'Yeah. Sorry.'

'And he just left it at that?' Cowley was stiff from sitting on the desk, listening to Bodie's report.

Bodie shrugged. 'He didn't make that much of it, and nor did I. "Seen her somewhere". That sort of thing. He quite fancied her, truth to tell. Got a thing for oriental girls has our Ray.' His face shadowed as the thought of Ray Doyle's punctured body made him realise that perhaps Doyle's oriental interests were a thing of the past, now.

Cowley said, 'And the place in Earl's Court. Charlie's bedsit. You turned it over?'

'It's in the report.'

'Now come on, Bodie. I don't want to be boring. I know you're tired. I know you're concerned about Doyle. But I want to hear it all. And I want to hear it from you. Just what did the two of you get up to?'

The caretaker was every bit the 'retired' hippy, forced to make a living. He smelled vaguely of jossticks, and his long, straggly hair was flecked with dandruff. He led the way up to the first landing, where Charlie had had his bedsit.

'Paid for a week. Stayed a week. Then took his stuff and went. Haven't had a chance to do anything to the room since. The cleaning girl's sick, and I like to trust my own, if you know what I mean.'

'Don't worry,' said Doyle. 'We're not thinking of renting. Did he give a name?'

'No name. And I didn't ask. His money was good enough.'

The room was large, sparsely furnished. It smelled damp, and there was the hint of wood smoke, left over from the illegal fire that Charlie had burned in the open grate. The cupboards were empty, of course. Doyle went to the fireplace and picked out a number of burned pieces of paper. Bodie upturned the waste bin and sorted through the small pile of chewing-gum wrappers, empty cigarette packets, and cigarette butts. There were a few pieces of wire among the rubbish, and he picked one up.

'Well, well. Fuse wire.' Doyle looked round from the fireplace.

'What a surprise,' he said. 'Anything else?'

Bodie had taken out the sheet of paper with which the waste-bin had been lined. He spread it out on the table and looked briefly at its incomprehensible, oriental symbols.

To the caretaker: 'You put this here?'

The man shook his head. 'Not me.'

'Would your cleaner have?'

'Shouldn't think so. What is it, Chinese or something?'

'Something like that.' Doyle came over and inspected the newspaper. Bodie added, 'It's the propaganda rag I mentioned. The one Latowa's Camden Lock friend produces.'

'Well, well, well,' said Doyle with a smile. 'Let's go and see him, shall we?'

'Maybe take out a subscription?'

'Chinese lessons first . . .'

Roddy Lou Thai was not pleased at all to be questioned by two representatives of the repressive Imperialist

Government, under whose chauvinistic wing he had been living for four years. He meant the United Kingdom. It took Doyle a moment to establish that fact.

Only the young man's intuitive fear of the heavy couple who had entered his shop, closed the door and locked it, and pushed him roughly into the back room, made him co-operate at all.

'What's happened to Latowa?' he asked, leaning against his desk. The desk was covered with copies of his propaganda news-sheet, and several colourfully produced pamphlets. His narrow, ugly eyes watched Bodie most of all, disliking the cut of the man, the touch of the 'hoodlum' that Bodie was so good at portraying.

'He didn't want to ask questions,' Bodie said softly. 'So he blew himself up.'

'You killed him,' challenged Thai, and turned a sweaty face to Doyle, who shook his head and smiled.

'We were only following him.'

'You were hounding him!'

Bodie said, 'It was him or a lot of other people.'

'And he didn't have to run,' Doyle added. 'So why did he come to see you?'

'When?'

'The day before he picked up Charlie.'

Thai was puzzled by that. 'Charlie?'

'The bomb maker!' said Doyle irritably. 'He also read your newspaper.' He took out the fragment of the news-sheet and waved it at Thai. 'We found it in his room, in Earl's Court.'

Bodie said, 'You had an argument with Latowa.'

'We saw you,' said Doyle. Thai's face turned frantically from one to the other of them, following the clipped words, the tough routine.

'What was it about?' pushed Bodie. 'What did he want from you?'

Thai stuttered nervously. 'He wanted me to pass on a message to the police. Warning people to get out of a certain hotel . . .'

'Did you?' asked Doyle, and Thai shook his head.

'I thought I'd persuaded him that he was being foolish.'

'Well you didn't,' snapped Bodie.

Thai said, 'Intellectually, I do not condone terrorism.'

'That's nice,' said Doyle sarcastically. 'How about emotionally? How about from the gut?'

'The men they wanted to kill were butchers.'

Doyle sniggered. 'Sure. Who was Charlie?'

Thai shrugged. 'I do not know any Charlie.'

'And if you did,' said Bodie tiredly, 'you'd grow old and die before you told us.'

'Let us say I might grow old and die trying to decide whether to act intellectually or emotionally.' Thai spoke without expression, but the sarcasm was clear.

'Inscrutable bastard,' Bodie said, as he and Doyle walked back to the car. Doyle was looking at the shop which sold oriental bits and pieces. The attractive owner could be seen, arranging items in the window.

'More junk?' Bodie asked.

'Just admiring a pretty pair of almond eyes.'

'You Inglis Johnnies all look alike to me,' mocked Bodie, as he got into the car.

A telephone began to ring as Bodie finished. Cowley just watched him implacably, then walked to the phone as Bodie said, 'We searched Latowa's place. Nothing. And that was it as far as we were concerned.'

Cowley had picked up the phone and was listening quietly. After a moment he said, 'I see. We'll be right over.' Replacing the phone he stared at it for a moment, then glanced at Bodie, who was waiting apprehensively for the news from the hospital. 'And Doyle never referred to the fact that he'd seen the Asian girl near to Charlie's?'

'No.'

'Was he giving up on the case?'

Bodie frowned. 'Why?'

'Doyle's taken a downward turn. That strength of will you say he has ... well, it doesn't seem to be working.'

'It will,' said Bodie, praying that he was right.

'The surgeon doesn't think he's trying.'

Bodie laughed ironically. 'I know what he means. Give Ray half a chance and he'd blame himself for the invention of gunpowder.'

But it was no laughing matter. Bodie stood by Doyle's bed and stared at the pale face of his friend, the eyes closed but moving restlessly beneath the lids.

Siegel stabbed a finger at the 'scope monitoring Doyle's neural activity. 'It's high, almost wild. There's a real battle going on inside his mind, but it seems that the battle is going the wrong way. His heart strength is fluctuating, but the average trend is downwards. The body is weakening. Adrenalin helps, but there's a limit to how much we can artificially stimulate the body.'

Bodie heard all this, let the words go into his mind, to shout at him, to make the blood in his body boil. Outwardly he remained calm.

He crouched by Doyle. 'Who was it? Who was it, Ray? Come on sunshine, pull through. Get it together, Doyle, or we'll never pin these bastards down ...'

'There's something happening ...' Siegel's voice cut through Bodie's whisper. Bodie glanced up, but all he could see were the same madly flickering lines, and slowly moving blips. Siegel looked at him. 'Did you just speak to him?'

'Just a few words of encouragement,' said Bodie.

'Heart strength jumped. A flurry of activity ...'

George Cowley stood silently staring at the unconscious man. Bodie put his lips close to Doyle's ear. 'Who was it, Ray? That editor bloke? The girl you saw? Who, Ray? Tell me who?'

And as he crouched there, quietly talking, so Doyle's right hand suddenly clenched and unclenched. The man's eyes did not open, but Bodie leaned back and watched the activity of the fingers. It looked as if Doyle was trying to grasp the sheet.

The nurse, watching the monitor screens, said, 'I'd say he showed all the signs of regaining consciousness. His heart beat is *very* strong, now.'

But Bodie heard no more from the medical staff. He was

watching as Doyle's index finger and thumb formed a circle, like an O, like a gesture of 'OK!' . . . a circle, like a ring . . . a ring . . .

Bodie rose to his feet, then quickly reached out to squeeze Doyle's hand. 'Got it, kid. Got it.'

Before Cowley could say a word, he had left the Intensive Care room and was pounding along the corridor to the front exit of the Hospital. In minutes he was driving, and soon was bursting into Doyle's flat, breathless from running up the stairs.

He went straight into the bedroom, to the wall where the painted Asiatic doll was perched on the sideboard. He snatched it up and tore the bronze ring from its wrist.

Holding the ring in his hand, he closed his fingers around it and squeezed.

'Bitch . . .' he said bitterly. 'Bloody bitch!'

## *Chapter Ten*

She picked up the phone before it could ring twice, and spoke softly into the mouthpiece. 'Mayli Koulo . . .'

Through the window she could see normal everyday activity around the lock. Below, in the shop, Sushi was working normally, unaware of the finality with which her partner was planning her last few hours in England.

'The Palace Hotel . . . Yes, I am ready. Thank you.'

She placed the receiver down and reached to the table top, picking up the silenced gun and holding it gently in both hands. She stared down at it, remembering the way she had used it just hours before, remembering the way it had kicked in her hand, bruising her flesh.

So quiet for something so deadly. The soft sound of the shots had knocked the man across the room, splashing his blood across a yard of wall. Had she killed him? She was sure that he could not have survived the shot to his heart. But memory of her weakness, of her unwillingness to shoot him one last, final time, made her feel sick to her stomach.

Today, when she went for Lin Foh, she would have to find a firmer resolve. The exiled oppressor of her people had to die, and she had to be sure of it.

She dressed quickly in slacks and a full-necked jumper. She slung a canvas bag over her shoulder, the gun inside it. With sun-glasses on her head, she looked like any other early-season tourist.

She was twenty-four years old. She left her shop and walked briskly from the area of the canal; to go and kill a prince.

In the CI5 computer room, Bodie reported what he had found out about the girl to Cowley.

'Name's Mayli Koulo. She's the daughter of a journalist,

an influential man. She has an arts degree from Sussex. In the last few hours she's moved house, but we'll find her. She doesn't seem to have been politically active, though her father was.'

Cowley leafed through the file that Bodie had gathered together on the girl. 'Arrested for sedition. Imprisoned without trial . . . by Lin Foh's bunch, of course. Escaped and fled to Amsterdam.'

Bodie nodded. 'That's where most of the refugees seem to have gathered. Strong ties with the South Moluccans.'

Cowley read a little more. 'Her father died in prison. Minister in Charge: Colonel Lin Foh, exiled after the revolution.' He looked up at Bodie, eyes narrowed. 'We've misunderstood the girl ... revenge is the motive, not politics. Revenge for the father's death, revenge for the death of her friends, which she links with Doyle.' He reached for the phone, placing the folder back on the table. 'Find out where Colonel Lin Foh is staying now, and get me Hogan at the Ministry. Tell him I'm on my way to see him.' He paused as the man at the other end said something, then asked, 'Any news on Doyle? No change? Thanks.'

He placed the phone down. Glanced up at Bodie: 'You've got work to do, Bodie. Ray Doyle will take care of himself.'

Mayli stepped confidently into the lobby of the plush hotel and looked quickly around. The lobby was quite full of people, all very elegantly dressed. A porter stood idly by the lifts. Behind the desk a single clerk busied himself with paperwork.

She bided her time, patiently seated in one of the comfortable chairs, reading a magazine. When the desk-clerk left his post for a moment, crossing to the lifts to talk to the porter, she moved quickly to the desk and left an envelope addressed to Colonel Lin Foh upon it.

When the clerk returned he saw the letter, glanced at the door, in an attempt to see who had left it, then slotted it neatly into one of the pigeon holes behind him.

Mayli walked by, smiling at the man, and glancing at the

pigeon-hole. Number 811. Eighth floor, room eleven.

She walked to the lift, smiled at the porter, and stepped inside. There was no lift-man, and when the doors closed she was alone, nervously watching as the light indicated the slow rise of the elevator.

At the eighth floor she stepped out into the corridor, glanced to the right ...

And froze!

Colonel Lin Foh, and two bodyguards, were just stepping into the adjacent lift. Before she could move, before she could think, the doors had closed and she was alone on the floor, her first opportunity missed.

Deciding against riding the lift back down, she walked to the stairs, and ran quickly down the eight flights.

At the bottom flight she walked more demurely, but when she came in sight of the lobby she stopped, watching as Lin Foh was addressed by the man she recognised from the car that had earlier pursued Latowa, and caused it to explode.

Again she hesitated. She could have drawn her gun, walked up to them all, and killed them all quickly. But even as she was unslinging her canvas bag, so the group moved off to the lifts again.

Bodie had arrived in the hotel lobby just after Lin Foh had left his room. Since the desk clerk was adamant that the Colonel had not left the hotel, Bodie took the letter addressed to Lin Foh, and offered to deliver it to him in person. When the lift doors opened and Lin Foh appeared, Bodie was waiting for him.

He acknowledged the CI5 man – Evans – who stood nonchalantly behind his charge, looking very slightly bored.

Lin Foh said, 'Ah. So you've been demoted to post-boy?'

Bodie just smiled as he handed the letter across. 'We've got grounds for believing that your life is in danger at the moment and ... '

Lin Foh reached out an arm and turned Bodie to walk with him. 'Tell it as we go,' he said. 'I'm late for an engagement.'

'I don't think you should go to your engagement,' Bodie

said softly. Lin Foh had opened his letter and stopped, staring perplexed at the blank sheet of paper that was inside it. 'What can this mean?' he said.

Bodie took the sheet from him and crumpled it up. 'It means that she now knows the number of your room. An old trick, but effective.'

'*Who* knows the number of my room?'

'A student called Mayli Koulo, daughter of – '

But Lin Foh interrupted him. 'Daughter of Doctor Koulo. I knew him well. But she's a student in Amsterdam. I'm sure of it . . . she's not in politics. She's not a terrorist.'

Bodie just said, 'Looks like someone made her into one. I wouldn't go to your engagement, if I were you. I'd go back to your room.'

And after a moment's searching hesitation, Lin Foh bowed slightly, turned, and obeyed.

At much the same time, George Cowley was being treated to a very fine Malt whisky by Peter Hogan, in Hogan's elegantly furnished office, in the heart of Whitehall. Hogan was a smooth, confident Foreign Office man, unflappable and oozing with reasonableness. Cowley sat stiffly in one of the leather armchairs, not at all happy with what Hogan had just told him.

'You mean to tell me, Peter, that you've always been aware of this spate of "reprisals" on officials of the fallen Government?'

'It's a weird situation, George. See it from our point of view. These people are not taking hostages, or causing any sort of trouble. The targets they're after are sort of their *own* people . . . '

Cowley was appalled. 'So what are you saying? We just let them kill whoever they want?'

'I'm saying,' said Hogan wearily, 'that it's a new kind of situation. We must clarify our attitude.'

'We *have* an attitude: to keep blood off the streets, to protect the life of our people.'

Hogan shrugged, tried to look placatory. 'George, you're wise enough in world affairs. The people who are now in power over there are the people we were trying to keep out.' He sipped his own Scotch. 'They don't like us very much.'

'And we're anxious for their friendship?'

'We certainly don't want to make unnecessary enemies – especially ones who could trigger off another Cambodia.'

Cowley shook his head, angrily stating, 'Dammit, Peter, they tried to kill one of my men.'

'I'm sure it won't happen again, George.' Before Cowley could voice his astonished irritation at that complacent comment, Hogan hurried on, 'It would have been altogether different if this Doyle of yours had died, believe me. We're lucky her aim was a little off. It seems she doesn't quite have the stomach to be an assassin.' Cowley watched him in disbelief. He could hardly credit the implications of what Hogan was saying. Hogan finished: 'They felt obliged to fill us in . . . '

'They?'

'Her Embassy.'

'Good God, man . . . but you didn't feel obliged to fill *me* in.' He rose to his feet.

Hogan looked slightly put out. 'I obviously should have briefed you, George, but I had no idea you'd do such a fast job on putting all this together.'

Cowley slammed his whisky glass down and rose, walking quickly to the door. 'Thank you,' he said angrily. 'I hope you'll enjoy reading about this in tomorrow's papers.'

'Read about what, George?' Hogan hastened to follow Cowley along the corridor, towards the exit. Cowley walked faster, swinging his coat over his shoulder. 'There's nothing to print,' Hogan protested.

'Our newspapers are fearless, Peter. They'll happily print rumour, hearsay, innuendo . . . '

'The facts are, George, that nobody gives a toss about that second rate little country!'

Cowley stopped abruptly and fixed Hogan with his coldest stare. 'But they'd care about Doyle, gunned down by an international terrorist. And an official spokesman who says "hands off, it won't happen again".'

'Your man's a faceless pig to most people out on the

streets,' said Hogan nastily, as Cowley led the way through the swing doors of the Ministry building, and hurried towards his chauffeur driven car, waiting for him at the bottom of the steps. 'They'd care as little about him as they cared about the two bombers who died in the van.'

Cowley reached his car, snatched the two way radio from the hands of his driver and called for Bodie.

Hogan shook his head wearily, exasperated by Cowley's quiet anger. 'All I'm saying, George, is that you shouldn't expect any help from us. At least not until we've worked out a policy with them.'

'Just let their targets sit back and wait for the bullet, eh?' Bodie came on the radio, confirming that Mayli Koulo had located Lin Foh's whereabouts.

'Thank you, three seven. I'll be in touch.' He handed the radio back to the driver, then turned back to Hogan. 'Do you know where Mayli Koulo is now?' Hogan shook his head. Cowley contemplated him for a moment, trying to decide whether or not the man was lying, then asked, 'What would you like us to do with her, once we've caught her?'

With a cynical little smirk, Hogan said, 'That rather depends on whether or not you've killed her. Which, off the record, George, I sincerely hope won't happen.'

'Or at least until we've worked out a policy.'

'Exactly.'

Cowley climbed into the back of the car, then leaned out the window to add, 'It seems that young Mayli has already located Colonel Lin Foh's new hotel. But don't worry about it. It also seems we got there first.'

The car slid away from the kerb, leaving a disgruntled, shaken Ministry man standing, watching the black limousine disappear into the traffic.

In the hotel lobby, Bodie came away from the desk and spoke briefly to Cowley. 'Three single women checked in yesterday. If she's sniffed out that CI5 are around, she may have checked out already.'

'Visit them all anyway,' said Cowley.

Bodie glanced around the lobby. A woman, intensely reading a magazine in the corner, gave him a quick thumbs up as she caught his gaze. The second clerk behind the desk was a man Bodie recognised as a new recruit to the forces of CI5. There was a third man, stationed outside.

'Going to be enough, d'you think?'

Cowley smiled thinly. 'It's going to have to be, Bodie.'

Quickly, then, Bodie checked the three rooms occupied by the three female arrivals. Two were still in, one of them young and obviously pleased to see Bodie. Bodie hesitated only briefly before making his apologies and walking away.

The third room had been occupied, and obviously deserted. The curtains were still pulled and the do-not-disturb sign was up on the door. Bodie sniffed the pillow: a hint of perfume.

She had been in the hotel, then. Perhaps she still was.

Acting with sublime incaution, Mayli struck later that same day. For several hours she had hidden in the service area, biding her time, finding her courage again. Then, by pure chance – but seeing it as an act of providence – she had heard Lin Foh call down for an early supper, for him and his CI5 guardian.

Watching from near the kitchens, Mayli had observed a trolley being made up, with cold foods, wine and coffee. She darted, out of sight, through the kitchens and to the service lift, remaining hidden until the white-jacketed waiter pushed the trolley past.

Faced with a silenced pistol, pointed unwaveringly at his head, and not knowing that the girl could not have pulled the trigger against an innocent man, he acceded to her demand ...

The waiter knocked hesitantly at the door of room 11, on the eighth floor. The CI5 man called from inside, 'Who is it?'

'Room service,' said the waiter, glancing down at the tip of the silencer he could see pointed at him from through the white cloth covering the lower part of the trolley.

The door to the room opened and Chris Evans glanced out, checked the identity of the waiter in his own mind, then peered both ways along the corridor.

When he was satisfied that all was clear, he stood back to let the waiter push the trolley into the room. He frowned as the waiter hesitated, then gasped with shock as the man, his nerve gone, fled away from the room.

The silenced gun spoke quickly from below the trolley. Evans was flung backwards, clutching his stomach, where bright red blood spurted between his fingers.

Quickly, Mayli stepped out from the trolley. She was sweating, and shaking very badly. She walked into the room, glancing only briefly at the shot CI5 man, who lay unconscious on the floor.

Colonel Lin Foh stepped from the bathroom, clad only in a towel around his waist. He saw Mayli, and stopped, his eyes widening, his lips parting as if he were about to speak.

Mayli hesitated just briefly before shooting him twice through the chest. The Colonel was flung back against the wall where he stood, for a moment, a puzzled expression on his face. He managed to murmur Mayli's name, then closed his eyes and slid down to the floor.

Mayli stared at him for just a second, then realised that the waiter would have given the alarm by now. She ran back into the corridor and back towards the service lift.

Behind her she heard Bodie's voice. He was racing up the stairs.

She entered the lift and impatiently pressed the button for the lower ground. Her heart was beating rapidly as she watched the floors wink by. The hand that held the gun was dripping with sweat, the metal feeling hot and slick.

When the lift doors opened she stepped quickly out into the wide service area, and began to run towards the door. A figure moved to her right, a man in overalls who suddenly braced his legs apart, and raised a gun.

'Hold it right there!'

Without thinking she snapped off a shot towards him, and through the blur of sweat in her eyes saw the figure spin, and lurch. A moment later she felt an agonising blow in her right shoulder, and was flung to the ground. Her ears stung with the booming echo of the shot.

Staggering to her feet she looked back towards the wounded man; he had slumped to the floor, and was trying to push himself back to a kneeling position.

She ran, oblivious of the pain in her body, and the warm flow of blood inside her clothes.

Out through the doors, into the descending gloom of dusk. There was her car, discreetly parked behind the dustbins. She weaved towards it, finding her vision blurring, her legs beginning to go weak.

She practically flung herself into the driver's seat, moaning loudly with pain as she eased herself into position and started the engine.

*A phone box! She had to find a phone box! Her friends would help her now.*

The last thing she saw as she lurched out of the kitchen yard, and through the gates, was Bodie's lean form, running into the yard behind her, and raising his pistol ...

Bodie snatched out his R/T and called Cowley. 'She's got wheels, now, a rented Mini Metro, white, licence number GLO 337X.'

'Are you mobile, three-seven?'

'Soon will be. Just get me a fix on that Metro ... '

Night fell, and Bodie was prowling the streets, searching for the girl, waiting for the call from Control to confirm that they had located her getaway car. He became impatient, frustrated; he kept seeing Ray Doyle's pallid features, reflecting the internal battle for survival that his friend was waging; he saw the sprawled corpse of Lin Foh, the gut shot Welshman, the wounded CI5 man in the basement.

For a girl with no 'stomach' to complete the assassination of Ray Doyle, she had proved remarkably adept at shooting an exiled Colonel and his bodyguard.

Heat of the moment, Bodie knew. It was very different from the cold-blooded killing of a man already down. She had run from the hotel, snapping off shots blindly; but the adrenalin in her body, the clarity of thought, the way her subconscious had controlled her actions, all of these things had sharpened her shooting to perfection ...

She had to be found. For so many reasons, she had to be found.

Bodie searched for an hour.

And then the call came through.

'She must have made her way to the East End to get to a phone box,' came the voice of Control. 'A panda car spotted her, slumped over the wheel, more dead than alive. But as they went to pick her up an Embassy limo intervened ... '

Bodie was too stunned to comment for a moment. Then he said loudly, '*What* Embassy ... ?'

'Her Embassy. They're claiming Diplomatic Immunity on her behalf ... '

'*What*?'

''Fraid so. She's an agent of the new Government, specifically hired to act as assassin against the exiled previous leaders.'

Bodie's car screeched through the London streets. A vision of Ray Doyle's shivering, bleeding body, shot three times purely for 'revenge', came to his mind. Cold anger made Bodie's face a mask of hatred, an evil, demonic mask, reflecting well the bitter anger inside.

'Where's the Embassy?' he asked softly. And Control told him.

By the time Bodie reached the dusk-lit Embassy in Kensington, the limousine had arrived at its front steps. Bodie left his car and walked towards it, watching as Mayli was helped from the car by two, black-suited men. She was being carried, almost, badly shot and very weak.

Bodie called out, 'Mayli Koulo!'

The two men helping her looked round in panic, and one of them left her side, drawing his gun. He stepped towards Bodie, his face a mask of oriental inscrutability, thin-lipped, narrow eyed, coldly unemotional. 'Get back!'

Bodie held his arms wide, showing that he carried no gun. Mayli looked round, blinking at him through sad, tired eyes.

Bodie called out, 'You're there, near as damn it. Home soil. I'm not paid to make any further waves.'

The Embassy man who held the gun didn't seem to understand, frowning as Bodie approached him, then taking a step backwards. Mayli just smiled thinly, weakly.

She knew why Bodie was here.

She knew everything. Including the fact that she was dying.

Bodie said, 'I just wanted to get a look at you before they spirit you away. I want to remember the face of the girl who coldly shot a policeman in the line of his duty.'

He stared at her, long and hard. She let him stare, let him take in her spirit, her strength, and her weakness.

When Bodie abruptly turned on his heel and went back to his car, she let her head drop slightly, and indicated that she should be helped on into the Embassy building.

Bodie sat in his car and called Cowley. 'What happens now?'

'Where is she? At the Embassy?'

'Just taken in.'

'How bad is she?'

'Hard to tell. Pretty badly shot; lost a lot of blood. Can't tell exactly. How about Doyle?'

'The hospital called me about half an hour ago,' Cowley said, and after a brief pause, 'Doyle regained consciousness at four this afternoon. He's going to be all right.'

For a few minutes, Bodie remained where he was, staring at the Embassy through the misting-up windscreen of his car, feeling relief flood his body like a tide. He kept smiling; he couldn't think why. But he also felt smug. He had *known* that Doyle would win the battle for life.

He had simply known it.

He was about to put the car in gear and drive to the hospital, when the door of the Embassy opened and there was a brief flurry of activity in the porchway.

Bodie leaned forward, puzzled. Something had been placed at the top of the steps, a human figure, bundled up in a blanket.

It took just a few instants for him to realise that the huddled figure was Mayli Koulo.

He got out of the car and began to walk towards the Embassy. A voice hailed him from a grille above the door.

'Mister Bodie, is it?'

Bodie stopped, frowning. 'Yes. Bodie.' The girl was making soft, whimpering sounds.

The voice said, 'Your people will want to tie up the loose ends. The girl is dying. It does not matter where a person dies; it matters only *why* they die. You may have her, Mister Bodie. Wherever she dies, she will be a martyr.'

'Bloody animals!' said Bodie loudly.

'Bloody pragmatists, Mister Bodie. That is all.'

Bodie went up the steps and stared down at the girl, who looked up at him pathetically.

Doyle's words came back to him. *A pretty pair of almond eyes.*

She looked so young, so helpless, this girl who had killed a man, and could have easily killed four.

But in this moment of confrontation, knowing that Ray Doyle would pull through, Bodie could not help but feel a touch of pity for the girl. To her country, to her Embassy, she was just a cipher, a functionary, a unit of assassination, to be dispensed with when its use was extinguished. She had done some terrible things, but unlike the cold fish of an editor, Roddy Lou Thai, she was not all intellectual, no emotion ...

She had attacked Ray Doyle because her heart had ached for her dead colleagues. That same heart had made her fire that last shot into the wall, and not into Doyle's brain ...

Bodie had to give her that.

He reached down and bundled her up into his arms, trying to drown the feeble cries of pain that she uttered, reassuring her that everything would be all right.

When the ambulance came, Bodie carried her from his car to the safe hands of the experts. As the ambulance weaved its way dramatically through the London night, Bodie sat with her, holding her cold, pale hand.

*The second time I've sat like this*, he thought, and allowed himself a wry smile.

The girl watched him through her pretty, almond eyes. The brightness in them was fading as death's dark cloak slowly wrapped around her.

The last thing she said was addressed to Bodie. 'How is your friend? The curly haired one?'

'He'll make it,' Bodie said, and strained to catch her dying words.

'I'm glad . . . '

When Bodie arrived at the hospital, first thing next morning, Ray Doyle was propped up in bed, looking as chirpy and as mischievous as ever. A drip still connected to his arm, and his flesh was sallow, but the old Ray Doyle sparkle was back in his eyes, and Bodie was glad to see it.

He came in carrying a bunch of black grapes, and sat down on the edge of the bed.

'How are you, Raymond?'

'Punctured,' said Doyle.

'Do you like black grapes?'

'Love 'em.'

'Me too,' said Bodie, and began to eat them.

After a moment, Doyle said, 'Cowley told me about the girl.'

'A pretty pair of almond eyes. She asked after you, just at the end.'

'How touching,' said Doyle coldly. 'How did you find out about her?'

Bodie grinned. 'You told me.'

Puzzled, Doyle shook his head. '*I* did?'

'Sort of. Whatever was going on in that head of yours, it was certainly dramatic.'

'Like a bad dream,' said Doyle. 'The shooting, her face, her eyes, the feeling of being dead. A vivid, very bad dream. A death dream, I suppose.'

'But you didn't die. I wouldn't let you.'

'I suppose I was technically dead when they were operating. From what Siegel tells me.'

Bodie shrugged. 'Yeah, OK. In that sense I suppose you did "die". For a few minutes.'

Doyle grinned, almost as if he was proud of that achievement. 'Well there you go. And I can tell you this. Having done it once, it won't be so bad the next time . . . '

# the trade

## william h. hallahan

'Puts William Hallahan up above Le Carré, Deighton and Co.'
*The Bookseller*

Journalist Bernie Parker didn't make a lot of sense that day. His words needed a bit of explanation. But Bernie is in no position to do that right now because he's just stopped several bullets outside a Paris metro. Bernie is dead. And no one knows what his last words mean.

The least Colin Thomas owes his late friend is a reason. As an international arms dealer scoring off the hotter edges of the cold war he has contacts. Contacts that lead him back to a ruthless and uninhibited woman and to the centre of a devastating plan to change the face of Europe – even if it means starting World War 3 – even if it means starting the countdown to doomsday . . .

ADVENTURE THRILLER 0 7221 4215 3 £1.75